The
VAMPiRE
GUiTAR

It's red but it aint paint

RICARDO X

ISBN 978-0-9569177-0-6

Published by Lewis and Holland

Gomer
Llandysul
Ceredigion

The author was born in Leeds. After attending Art School and joining the BBC he worked as an editor, director and producer. He went on to set up his own television production company in Wales and after a stint as a University lecturer he decided to become a moped mechanic. His previous book, Talking Stones, was published by Gomer.
Discover more on the website.

www. vampireguitar.com

It all began as a screenplay

with

An Ear for Music ♫
A Throat for the Guitar

ONE

When Sir Lancelot Walters Wynn murdered his wife for her infidelity, his mother in law for having given birth to his wife and his children for having been born to his wife he knew he was doomed. He killed himself by leaping off a tower. As he hurtled to the ground he misjudged his descent and was impaled on the railings below and his bloated and ruddy corpse was laid to rest as close to the churchyard as his executors could arrange. Sir Lancelot's contemporaries believed that suicide was an unforgivable sin and that such tortured souls were unable to rest in their graves. Others believed that these bodies could not decay and turn to dust and that they left their coffins at night to torment the living. No proper consent could be gained for placing Sir Lancelot's body in hallowed ground so he was buried by a small grey alder tree within sight of his great house.

As the alder tree grew it fought with the elements. If there was a warm wind its branches hissed and assaulted the balmy air. It shuddered and moaned if there was soft rain though all other alders loved water. The tree was only content during a storm when it could poke and stab at passing clouds. It quarrelled with the sun and even a gentle heat would agitate the tree making its bark quiver irritably. Years later when a virgin gypsy horse cantered close to Sir Lancelot's grave the young stallion balked as he approached the site and badgers who hunted for nocturnal treats by scratching at the earth would always leap over the disturbed ground. During the late spring the tree produced catkins which left a foul taste in the mouths of birds that dared to try the fruits. In summer, the leaves rustled menacingly when people walked past on their way to church and as the alder matured its roots grew into grasping greedy tentacles that possessed the coffin…but really it was the coffin that possessed the tree.

TWO

AUTUMN 1974

Wrexford's open air market was about to close for the day. The sharp wind that was blowing stall canopies about like sheets on a washing line had kept most people at home. Two men walked hurriedly past the market traders and ignored their desperate overtures. They did not want packs of tools, cheap underwear or mongrel puppies. Frankie, a young man in a fringed jacket and sideboards shaved to look like cleavers, suddenly stopped. He had found the stall he was looking for. He turned to his friend.

'This would make an amazing shirt.'

'Bit loud isn't it?' said Sticky, who was a little older than his mate. Sticky wore a trademark creased leather waistcoat and pointed shoes. Frankie's eyes wandered over the gaudy fabric.

'No one else wears this kind of stuff.'

Great splashes of orange and yellow covered the heavy black wool.

'How much would I need to make up a shirt?' Frankie asked the trader.

'It's household fabric son. What do you want a shirt from this for?' The trader sucked on his cigarette.

'He's going into show biz,' Sticky hinted.

'What! As a curtain?' The trader laughed then handed Frankie a short roll of fabric.

'Two quid to you pal and it's dry clean only.'

The two friends took the wrapped cloth and hurried off before the storm moved in for the kill.

During the night, the weather seemed to bear a grudge against the world. After a few hours of metrological madness a nervous badger emerged from a hole in the ground. It took one look at the frenzied air and immediately returned to the safety of its subterranean home. Strong winds howled through the woods, shaking branches and blasting leaves into the inky void as they beat everything into a pulp. The huge alder tree, near the churchyard, was riddled with age and was weakening. Lashed by the demented air it began to creak and bend in the gale. The earth around its roots broke up as the tree rocked back and forth in a macabre dance that twisted the entrails of the giant alder in the loosened soil. Then with a shattering sound that deafened and terrified the night creatures the tree's trunk split open and leaned over heavily. As the tree roots became exposed the badgers, who normally do not see very much, noticed that the alder's wiry toes gripped the remains of a heavily carved coffin.

With a final lurch the mighty alder tree crashed to the ground and crushed the casket trapped beneath it. Fragments of carved wood and iron clasps were flung out amongst the broken branches and earth. As the storm died down the badgers left their sett. They were homeless now.

The high grey stone walls of an ancient college, built from the remains of Sir Lancelot Walters Wynn's ancestral pile, kept out the worst of the gale. Dark shapes, illuminated and thrown by iron lamp posts, fell on the surface of the limestone like giant animated fingers. A few leaves were blown about as Bramble, the night porter, made his tour of the quadrangle. He was rather self-important and regarded these nightly rounds like an act of national security. Using his rolled up umbrella he struck aside disorderly twigs from his immaculate pathways. His rotund and heavy body was stuffed into the suit cum uniform that college servants at older universities had to wear. As Bramble adjusted the little gap between the tight collar and his bulging neck muscles he stopped to look at the clouds as they scudded past the moon. Above him the library, closed for some hours now, caught a little light from the lamp posts.

Inside the building long rows of beautifully carved cabinets and shelves stood by like regiments dedicated to knowledge. Near the south east oriel window, where the oldest books were kept, the leather bound volumes glinted in the night as the lamplight reflected off their covers. Suddenly the sheen of the books was broken by the shadow of a hooded figure as it moved past them. The figure stopped at a dusty section and began to search frantically through a heavy volume. Finding the light level low the hooded one turned and groped until it found a switch on a small table lamp. The light cast a weak and intermittent glow over the shelves as the figure hurriedly turned over the stained pages. A couple of heartbeats later some hurried footsteps could just be heard in the distance. The hooded one put back the book it was holding and grabbed at another. The footsteps were getting closer. The second book was returned to its shelf and the figure snatched at a third and opened it urgently. A long finger nail scanned the faded manuscript as the door burst open and the main room light was switched on. Bramble was puffing like an old steam train after his ascent of the staircase. He croaked out a warning.

'Don't move! The police have been called and they're on their way!'

The figure froze as it heard the sound of an approaching patrol car. Its blue light just registered on the window panes.

'What's your business here?' called out Bramble.

The hooded figure turned to face the night porter. Bramble steeled himself and raised his rolled up umbrella. The hood was lowered and Bramble spat out a note of recognition.

'Professor Van Hellbent Junior! I'm sorry. I didn't realise it was you sir.'

'That's alright Bramble. I was just on my way to a fancy dress party and wanted to check the historical accuracy of my costume. Fourteenth century Fakirs wore a particular type of cloak you know.'

Seeing Brambles's expression cloud over, Van Hellbent added.

'Er…they were Eastern mystics.'

Bramble who was embarrassed made up for lost ground.

'Of course sir. I mustn't act with such alarm next time I see a strange light on in the very valuable and irreplaceable old manuscript room. I beg your pardon sir.'

Van Hellbent turned back to his books. He had crow black hair that lay in masses of curls and there was a strange sparkle in his eyes. In an earlier age he would have been the type of man that managers of grand hotels and posh waiters respected. Hellbent was young for a professor of Medieval Folk History. He had a brilliant and inquiring mind and came from a long line of academics that specialised in myths and legends.

Despite the interruption he was already back to his reference works. Happy that all was as it should be, Bramble backed out of the room but immediately reappeared at the head of a stampede of policemen. One of them was in plain clothes.

'I'm Inspector Smollett. Right what's goin' on 'ere then? Who's the mad intruder in the blanket?'

Bramble shifted towards the officer and tried to play the diplomat.

'Ah... Professor Van Hellbent Junior was doing some unscheduled research Inspector and I'm afraid that I acted rather hastily.'

The Professor turned a page and without looking up from the book confirmed Bramble's explanation.

'That's right Inspector. I was just checking on the historical accuracy of my costume when I was disturbed...'

'Checking your costume! Don't you realise police time is valuable gentlemen? We could have been saving lives, apprehending bank robbers or collecting sandwiches from the corner shop in a car with flashing lights instead of wasting tax payers money on you academics.'

Inspector Smollett was in his late forties. His most distinctive feature was his thin moustache which with his slicked back hair made him look like a band leader from a 1940s film. It was his way of hinting that he had a bit of style despite the often grim demands of his detective work. It was a job that had seen him languish in the middle ranks for too long. He felt his moment had passed and it would take a major crime solving success to bring him to the attention of his superiors.

Smollett looked around the library and decided he had lost enough time. There was no path to glory here. He gathered his men and left muttering about false alarms. The heavy door slammed as they went.

THREE

A few miles to the north of the university a forest had been hammered by the storm. Most of the havoc involved broken branches and some shallow rooted trees had been torn up. But that was not all. When the morning sun broke through the clouds it shone on a road running below the tree line. The view from the top of a hill revealed the fallen alder lying across the tarmac. In the near distance a dark blue truck chugged its way towards the smashed tree. It was a dangerous obstruction and had to be removed.

The truck reversed away from the tarmac onto a patch of grass at the edge of the forest. As the ground was still soft the driver made sure he had his nearside tyres on the road. Stoutly built lumberjacks with loud voices crawled over the fallen alder and attached chains and hacked off awkward limbs. They cut up and loaded the broken timbers that lay across the highway but they failed to notice the remains of the splintered coffin among the bushes. Using a small crane on the back of the logging truck the great alder was hoisted onto the trailer platform. When the men finally cleaned up the road they climbed into the truck and pulled away. As the vehicle moved off some mud fell from the base of the tree to reveal a dark red stain.

From an eagle's high vantage point the logging truck groaned along the forest road with a noisy change of gear as it climbed round a hairpin bend. The mighty bird of prey took off and tracked the logging team then veered back to its crag. Behind the ivy clad rock, where the bird had made its nest, were the towers of an overgrown ruin.

A few miles away, Professor Van Hellbent Junior was in a

fevered state. His eyes were closed and he was shaking so much that the test tube in his hand fell from his grasp and hit a stained parquet floor. The sound of the breaking glass woke him with a start. He gazed at his surroundings but they appeared in soft focus. Just as he began to recognise the university science room two men in white lab coats appeared. One of them demanded an explanation.

'What on earth are you doing here Van Hellbent…Junior?'

The Junior part of the name was oddly emphasised.

'Don't you know this is a highly sensitive area. You haven't taken up industrial espionage have you? Working for the Plastic Banana Company are we now?'

'Oh Professor Vasseline,' replied Hellbent in a drowsy voice.

'I.. er...apologies for entering your lab uninvited. I don't know what came over me. Please excuse me.'

Hellbent slid past both men and stuttered as he left.

'I mmmust return to my chambers. If there's any damage please charge it to me personally.'

Professor Vasseline screwed up his face. He was a skinny man pushing sixty with translucent skin and narrow piercing eyes which made him look like he was squinting at a bright object. He turned to his young assistant.

'Odd character…just like his great great uncle. Must be a family trait.'

'Who was his great great uncle?' asked the younger man.

'Ah… August Van Hellbent,' replied Vaseline, 'He was a highly respected academic and an investigator of the supernatural. He had a brilliant mind. Specialised in the undead you know.'

'What... Vampires!'

'Yes...chilling thought isn't it. But he really believed in the power of ancient folk tales.'

The young assistant looked dismayed.

'But blood sucking demons....'

Professor Vasseline examined some apparatus for damage and looked back.

'They may be fearful dreams to you and I, but the Van Hellbents have made them a family speciality. Demons, werewolves, witches, hobgoblins and superstition are their stock in trade. Van Hellbent Junior is obsessed by it all.'

'How do you mean Professor?'

Vasseline ignored the young man and anxiously checked the contents of his desk. It was as if he had something to hide and it was not just the trespasser in his lab that was making him jittery.

'Are you alright Professor? I mean Van Hellbent only broke an empty test tube.'

'Mmmh ...yes I know but my work is so important. I really cannot have it disturbed by anyone.' The Professor was quite agitated now.

'Especially by that fool.'

'Of course!' snapped the assistant agreeing with Vasseline.

The Professor turned and smiled at the young man. No one had disturbed the contents of his desk and he decided to be a little friendlier. After all the assistant was only trying to ingratiate himself with one of the greatest scientific minds that the university ever had.

'Hellbent Junior, has occasional attacks of dislocation. He ends up in various places, usually in some ridiculous costume. It's as if he's engaged on some search for an answer to a riddle that he can't quite put his finger on. Certainty wasn't poor old Augustus's style.'

'You mean...'

'Yes...Van Hellbent Junior is as mad as a hatter's ferret.'

FOUR

Along the lower reaches of the river Deep were the remains of old quaysides. The mud banks had not been cut back for years and the area was turning to marshland. Here on the Anglo Welsh border were the industrial estates of Wrexford. Some engineering works still hung on but the industry had contracted. What was left was lean. On a small estate to the west a couple of units were making furniture from compressed wood chippings and providing space for companies making birthday cards and party decorations. Amongst the corrugated line of grey sheds was a large pink neon sign. It was loosely in the shape of a Fender Stratocaster guitar crossed with a small horned Gibson SG and it dominated one corner of the site.

A fork lift truck shifted a recently delivered alder tree that had been brought down in a storm. It had been stripped of its mottled mossy bark and dried. It was now ready for cutting. The driver took the tree trunk inside the factory with the neon sign. Under soft strip lighting a dozen toilers worked by their benches. Machine-cut guitar parts were being assembled into recognisable shapes with the addition of metal components. Pick-ups that amplified the sound of wire strings and machine heads to tighten them were being fixed into position. On a cutting machine a new block of wood was waiting to be shaped. The block had a curious red stain in its centre. Lying on a bench next to it a freshly cut guitar body had a red stain on it too. This was not a problem as all the guitars were going to be painted. Raised voices caused one of the workers to look up to an elevated office and smile knowingly. *They* were at it again.

In the manager's office two men were arguing. One was

middle aged, balding and obviously enjoyed his pint judging by the size of his paunch. The other was in his early twenties and was wearing a shirt so florid and brightly coloured it made your eyes ache. The woollen fabric that had started out as curtain material had been turned into a fashion item. The older man was the factory boss and his adversary was his brother in law. Both of them were wrung out with the emotion of their quarrel. The boss was doing most of the talking. Though they were on the Welsh side of the border they spoke with a North Country twang which was common hereabouts.

'I've never known anyone as lazy, as unpunctual, as unreliable and as dishonest a worker as you Frankie. You're a bloody disgrace. Well yer shirt is anyway,' he was warming up, 'And as for pulling yer weight! It takes you an hour to get to work…and that's after you get 'ere.'

Frankie stared out onto the factory below and replied grudgingly.

'You've got room to talk Gordon.'

The older man choked. 'Listen mate…if brains were dynamite you wouldn't have enough to blow yer own nose.'

Frankie exploded, 'Hang on! You only got this business 'cos me sister was a widow and she couldn't manage the factory on her own.'

'Hey…ya little prick! I'm a successful businessman in my own right and I'll 'ave you know I'm the most respected guitar collector ever.'

Frankie's jaw dropped. He raised the stakes.

'My poor sister must 'ave been blind drunk and cock-eyed when she met you.'

Gordon clenched his fists.

'Well thank you Doctor Freud. D'ya know I've developed an attachment for you pal and I'm gonna fit it over yer dirty little mouth. Come 'ere.'

Gordon lunged at Frankie missed and then chased him around the office.

Frankie started for the door and shouted back.

'You can stuff the job. Who wants to paint the canteen walls when I should be in the drawing office designin' proper guitars. I know what's what.'

Gordon scoffed.

'Christ! If scientists were inventing idiots they'd use you as a blueprint.'

As Frankie went through the door he couldn't resist a parting shot.

'I don't know what makes you tick fat arse but I hope it's a bomb.'

Gordon threw a phone directory at Frankie as the youngster bolted out onto the staircase.

Frankie marched purposefully towards the locker room. As he arrived the factory foreman watched over him as he emptied his possessions into a canvas bag. The troublemaker was escorted out of the works and through a narrow corridor. A trolley packed with boxes was being pushed in the opposite direction by an office junior. As they converged the boxes caught on the wall's skirting board and tumbled to the floor. The foreman helped the young girl pick up her cargo leaving Frankie standing next to a large key box which had a torch lying on top of it. The foreman good humouredly told the girl that it was the wall's fault for squeezing in on her.

The Black Cat, an old Tudor style pub painted in the usual black and white style offered a refuge of sorts. It was just beyond the industrial estate and Frankie sat inside drinking alone. It must have been an inspirational brew because he soon took out a pen and began to doodle on the back of a beer mat. He drew a stylised guitar. Then he drew several guitars on several beer mats and seemed oblivious to the day turning into night.

Meanwhile, at the ancient university there was a special function taking place. In fact the ancient university was not really that ancient. Only Oxford and Cambridge were really old but it was built at a time when the Victorians had a love affair with all things gothic. So it had castellations, towers, arched windows and a grand hall. It was a romantic copy of a castle and gave the university a kind of aristocratic pedigree. That pedigree was about to be challenged. Professor Van Hellbent Junior lurched down a corridor near his university chambers. His eyes were glazed and he was vaguely aware of a noisy social whirl taking place just ahead of him.

At the Black Cat, Frankie sat behind a row of empty beer glasses raised his drowsy head and asked the landlord for a drink in a mock theatrical voice.

'Another glass of Old Peculier if you will tavern keeper.'

The landlord turned to his stock of bottled beer and clanged about for the requested ale. Frankie reached into his jacket pocket and fished about for some money but as his hand came out something fell onto the floor. There was a metallic clatter that made him look down. It was a factory key. He smiled wickedly and tub-thumped his still empty glass on the table.

Van Hellbent Junior weaved his way in the direction of a distant crowd. As he stepped through a grand doorway he lost his footing and was shaken out of his trance. He found himself carrying a tray stacked with vol-au-vents serving the guests at the Principal's Dinner. It was a black tie affair. Suddenly seeing himself reflected in a mirror, Van Hellbent's blood ran cold. He was dressed as a showgirl! A glittery, high-heeled hoofer in fishnet tights and sparkly burlesque top. Van Hellbent Junior looked around in despair. There was no hiding place.

Outside the Deepside industrial estate Frankie crept between two buildings. He knew a back way onto the guitar factory site. He looked over his shoulder to make sure he was alone and moved slowly towards a side door. Taking the key out of his pocket he aimed for the lock. Three attempts later he was in. Despite his boozy state Frankie knew his way around. He managed to turn off the simple lever alarm system, picked up the torch near the key box and weaved his way into the production area. With the aid of the beam he found what he was looking for. He popped the torch into his mouth to free up his hands and started to collect the various bright metal components that he wanted. Three pick-ups, some machine heads, a tremolo arm, a jack plug and a finished and fretted guitar neck. He put them all into his canvas bag.

The college porter, Bramble, danced past senior members of the University and pirouetted through the tight gaps between the dining tables. He came up alongside Van Hellbent Junior.

'Now sir, shall we go this way? I'm sure the good professor would like some fresh air.'

As he gripped Van Hellbent, *the showgirl*, lowered his head and whispered.

'Do you know Bramble I'm beginning to worry about the frequency of these attacks. Something must be up.'

Bramble looked around and shoved Van Hellbent along.

'Quite sir, but let's not disturb the other guests. There's a good chap.'

As they moved between the diners they overheard some tut tutting.

'Not the sort of thing you'd expect of a Van Hellbent.'

'Bloody disgrace!'

'It's an affront to his great great uncles's memory.'

'He's not dangerous is he?'

At the guitar factory, Frankie picked up a piece of the stained alder wood that was already cut into a slab from the forest trunk. He placed it in a shaping machine and started to carve. He was guided by his drawing on a creased beer mat. A series of curves and two horns began to emerge. He was making his own guitar body. The design was loosely based on a classic Stratocaster but the horns that would allow his hands to work the neck were more extreme and the body was sharply waisted in the centre. When the wood was cut to his near satisfaction Frankie turned off the machine and sanded down the edges. He was unhappy with one of the horns and picked up a craft knife to gouge out a sharper tip. As he guided the blade with his free hand he pushed it forward almost parallel to the wooden body. Just as he rounded off the horn point he pushed the knife blade too far and nicked a finger.

'Shit and bollocks!!'

He sucked his finger to soothe the pain and the hurt seemed to sharpen his senses. He realised he was doing something he should not be doing and decided to leave quickly. As he lowered his hand to pick up the guitar body a droplet of blood fell onto the wood. It landed on the red stain which momentarily expanded then seemed to breathe before it shrank to its former size.

Over at the Principal's Dinner, Van Hellbent and Bramble passed from the dining room into a foyer. Above them was a portrait in oils of an eminent looking gentleman. Apart from the monocle and Victorian period whiskers there was a strong resemblance to Van Hellbent Junior. It was a picture of August Van Hellbent, his great great uncle. The painting depicted a strongly built man with a noble head and bushy eyebrows. It was said that August knew what he was talking about better than anyone else. He was a philosopher, historian and one of the most advanced scientists of his day. He knew about obscure diseases, ancient remedies, myths and legends, new technologies and he had the truest of hearts. He also had a large nose which was the only thing not passed on to his great great nephew.

FIVE

The sixties development of council housing in Wrexford produced some tower blocks that stood out from the Victorian heart of the city like immense jackboots. It was late and just a few lights were on in the apartments occupied by the unemployed or retired. Late night television kept them from their sleep and as they did not need to rise early the next morning they lived by their own schedules. They only went to bed when their storage heaters shut down.

The door of Frankie's flat still had the claw marks of the previous tenant's dog. The original blue paint was faded and from the evidence around the lock the door had been forced at some stage in its life. Inside, the accommodation was generous enough but tired looking wallpaper and a carpet with a pattern that looked like pies had been thrown at it suggested that the current resident had his mind set on other things. Frankie sat on his sofa with his guitar body laid flat across his lap. He had already fitted the maple neck to the guitar and was fixing three electro magnetic pick ups to the body. He had not bothered with the usual plastic pick guard as he intended to build up the guitar first and test it. With the machine heads fitted Frankie tightened up his wire strings. Noticing that one of his pick-ups was not angled correctly Frankie loosened it off and re-aligned it. As he adjusted its position with a fine bladed screwdriver he accidentally jabbed his finger and a drop of blood fell onto the guitar. He cursed and as he sucked on his wounded digit he thought back to the cut he gave himself in the factory. This guitar building lark was proving hazardous.

As he wet his finger with saliva there was a growing chill

in the room and what seemed like a faint moan coming from somewhere. Frankie thought about turning in for the night. It was late even for him and the beer was taking its toll, not to mention the stress of the break-in. As he considered his options the moan became more tremulous and haunting. It was as if he was being called by an unseen spirit. He looked around the empty room then shook his head nervously. A vision of a dark forest and a thin red mist rolling towards him made him more uneasy and that moaning sound came up again. He shuddered a little. It was time to curl up.

He raised the guitar one last time to check the instrument was straight and placed the base of the body against his neck. As he looked along the bridge past the tremolo arm and up to the frets he thought he heard the strange moan again. He lowered his head towards the guitar body. Where was that noise coming from? Was it a hum on the wire strings? Frankie looked up the length of the guitar. The machine heads, the oval shaped knobs at the top of the neck, appeared to turn slowly of their own accord! How could that be? Frankie's eyes widened and became fixated on the action. The machine heads were now turning anti-clockwise, slackening the strings and picking up speed. Frankie was mesmerised and startled by the motion. The moaning sound was intensifying too. It was distorting and swirling around penetrating his ears and nose and his hair. His pupils reflected the bright steel of the loosening wires and widened in horror as they threw themselves at him.

Frankie felt the hot pain. It coursed through his veins and his head felt as though it was being squeezed in a massive spiked vice. He struggled to his feet and tried to tear himself away from the guitar but the strings had wrapped themselves around his body and tightened up around his neck. He writhed and rolled like a wreck on a rocky shore but it was hopeless. He felt more fear and slicing pain than he had ever known and he tried to scream but only gasps came from his lacerated throat. His youthful flesh was being drained of the last drops of his life blood. He died when his heart gave up.

Vampires, the undead, the evil immortals and all those who inhabited and dominated the twilight zone usually took their blood in instalments. After a few days their prey became like their masters and then they too found new victims. If all the blood was taken at once the victim died. The guitar was a killer.

Outside on the city street the emerging light brought out the road cleaners and early commuters. A little later, Sticky, the crony in the creased waistcoat who'd been with Frankie at the open-air market, stepped out of a newspaper shop. He made his way across the road and entered Frankie's apartment block. Sticky was a roadie and worked in the music business but he had a sideline. He was a pusher. His drug of choice was made from the finest horseradish money could buy. Sticky took the lift up to the fifth floor and walked out onto an open corridor. He saw a row of blue doors and stopped at the second one along and knocked. He hammered several times but there was no answer. He bent down and peered through the letter box.

'Frankie, it's me, Sticky. Open up,' his voice was hoarse.

There was no reply.

'Look I know you're in. Come on pal.'

There was still no reply. Sticky waited a minute then tried the door handle. You never know. The door opened and he entered cautiously, careful not to catch his cuban heels on the worn mat. As it was early he was pretty sure lazy bones Frankie would still be in bed. He moved along the hallway towards the bedroom just past an untidy and sour smelling bathroom.

'Frankie…you still out of it? Come on sleepy head. I bet yer washing dishes in bed again…Frannnkee.'

He slowly pushed on the door to the bedroom. The curtains

were open but there was no sign of Frankie. Strangely, the bed looked as if it had not been slept in and the pillows looked almost neat.

Sticky turned back into the corridor and moved into the lounge. The curtains here were still drawn and the room was in half-light.

'Frankie…where are you mate. Just want a few quid like… come on.' He was beginning to sound indignant.

'You promised to pay today…Gordon takes care of you don't he? I've gotta buy more sauce.'

There was no reply. Sticky moved slowly across the carpet towards the back of the sofa then his world imploded. He was falling fast. He came down hard and banged his knee. Damn! He had tripped over a guitar and crashed to the floor. Recovering from the fall he turned and his head and came face to face with Frankie's slashed and blood congealed throat. He screamed out loud then stopped himself. Sticky didn't leave empty handed.

Outside the block of flats the squad cars arrived at speed. The mystery caller had been quite certain about the location of the body. Inspector Smollett, who had had very few interesting cases lately, stared excitedly at the corpse. His team were busy taking away the evidence, rifling through the kitchen and looking inside various drawers. Smollet squatted by Frankie's poor body.

'So…he appears to have topped himself in some way. Maybe he was depressed after losing his job? Maybe he had girlfriend trouble?'

He squinted at Frankie's throat.

'Maybe…he cut himself shaving with a chisel?'

Smollett looked over the body but failed to notice a distinctive mark on Frankie's torn neck. Under a coating of dry blood there was the feint outline of a little guitar mark with horns.

SIX

Grimwade's was a secondhand shop that stocked junk of all sorts. Picture frames hung from the ceiling along with dusty stringed instruments and matt finished trumpets and trays. Most of these items had seen better days and customers had to negotiate various mine detectors, chests and small items of furniture to get to the counter. The good stuff lay in glass cabinets covered in greasy fingerprints. Here bits of jewellery, watches, rings and brooches lay on sheets of tissue paper. A guitar was laid flat on top of one of these cabinets.

'What'll you give us for it then?' demanded Sticky.

The shop owner was used to this direct approach. This was no place for beating about the bush. He looked at the guitar and lifted it closer.

'Well it's got a weird finish on it. Looks just half painted to me. Bright red over part of the body and half bare wood. It's not gonna be worth much in that state. Tell you what, I can scrape up twenty quid but that's it. Top whack and I'm doin' you a favour.'

Sticky looked resigned.

'Look I'm a bit short this week.'

'Oh legless are we?' Grimwade sniggered. Then he leant forward, his large stomach pushing against the side of the guitar. He looked at Sticky as if he were an insect and after a pause made his mind up.

'Well its still twenty quid...take it or leave it.'

Sticky raised his hand grudgingly.

The guitar hung about in the shop window for a few days. Grimwade knew that come Friday there would be some interest in it. Pay day guaranteed the fact. Over the weekend a succession of would be buyers tried out the guitar. All of them suffered from cut fingers after playing just a few notes. One by one they walked away. After the last customer, a long-haired lad in pinstriped jeans tried his luck Grimwade moved in for the kill.

'So what do you think mate? Serious rock 'n' roll tackle or what?'

The young customer pulled his shoulders back at the dubious claim.

'I wouldn't have it thrown at me. It sounds crap and the strings are like razor blades. Ya need a pair of gloves to play it. And that paint finish! I saw it in the window a couple of days ago and it's faded since.' Grimwade sucked through his teeth.

'Tell you what pal, fifty quid 'cos I think you've got talent and you could do with a break.'

The long haired youth shoved the guitar into Grimwade's stomach and moved off.

'Yeah, I'll break me hand playing it too. No thanks.'

As the lad walked away Grimwade slapped a forty pound sticker on the guitar. Soon after, a young woman with dyed red hair the colour of a Ferrari sportster came in. Grimwade eyed her up and held up the increasingly pale guitar.

'It's just come in. The lad that's just left has had to let it go. Somethin' to do with the Child Support Courts. He was desperate. I'm not makin' anythin' on it.' She looked interested.

SEVEN

The sound of heavy metal riffs drifted out of a splintered door in an alleyway. Vivid signs declaring radiator repairs and gearbox rebuilds indicated the kind of craft skills that lay beyond the portals in this sturdy old part of the city. Except for one. This door had the name of a band painted freehand over the burst paintwork. This was the home of The Cerys Clark Three.

Inside, the young woman from the junk shop played her newly acquired guitar. She had bought a mottled guard to fit over the pick-ups and it gave the guitar an unusual look. The redhead wore studded suede gloves with the fingers exposed as she plucked away. She pinched, hammered and demonstrated a few pull offs to her band mates who listened intently. When she had finished she looked up.

'Good or what?'

A roadie who sat on some cable boxes spoke first. He was older than the rest of them and that fact gave him some authority. Plus he bought the chocolate digestive biscuits that had been their early supper.

'That guitar looks a bit past it Cerys,' he said. 'Thought you wanted a shiny red one?'

'Well Sticky it is kinda red. Must be the light in here that gives it a funny look.'

He had not recognised the guitar. It was paler than when he had sold it and the mottled pick guard made a difference too.

The drummer, a good looking twenty year old with checked flared trousers, long blonde hair and a goatie beard stood up.

'I reckon Sticky's been overdosin' on his sauce and can't tell what colour anything is.'

Sticky had begun to smear his forearm with a thick white paste and inhaled.

'Best horseradish you can get Dylan. Here try some of this.'

He passed round an open jar for the band to sniff. The keyboard player, Brian, looked on disapprovingly

'Don't forget we're playing tomorrow tonight.' He reminded them mockingly.

The others sniffed away and ignored him. Sticky had scientific information to pass on.

'You play better when you're on the horseradish Brian. Go mad like.'

The keyboard player looked at him in disbelief.

'How would you know…you're tone deaf.'

Dylan, joined in.

'Yeah…you can't play a note.'

Cerys went up to Sticky and gave him a hug.

'Trouble with you Sticky is you don't just suffer from insanity. You enjoy it.'

Sticky grunted

'Hey, so like who's the brains of the organisation? Who got tomorrow night's job?'

Cerys raised her eyebrows in mock respect and replied with a bone-jarring chord that reverberated down the alleyway. She had a suggestion too.

'You're right. So let's go for a drink guys. It's Horror Night at the Cat tonight.'

The Cerys Clark Three plus one took off down the alleyway and turned a corner in their old van.

The Black Cat occupied a high point overlooking Wrexford. It was the last pub before open countryside stretched out to the misty slate hills in the distance. When the band arrived they parked outside the back door of the old coaching inn. There was a graveyard and church next door and beyond that the ruins of a grand old mansion. Dylan, the drummer wanted to restore the old house when he made his million dollar album.

The band trotted across the freezing car park and made for the massive wooden door of the ancient boozer. The lounge area was half-timbered and had a roaring log fire. It was a good setting for the landlord's Horror Night. The place was almost full and customers propped up the bar and crowded around the tiny stage. Miraculously, there was a small table still available in one corner. The band made a beeline for it while Sticky grabbed a spare stool. With the band in place Sticky returned to the bar and bought the drinks.

As the stage was being set Dylan put his arm around Cerys and leaned forward.

'Last night I took Cerys home from a party. I placed her head on my shoulder…'

Brian joined in.

'Yeah and I carried her feet!'

Sticky laughed and Cerys poked Dylan in his ribs. It was going to be a good night. A bell rang out. There was an announcement from big Al, the landlord. He was a well-built man with a bushy set of whiskers. His booking policy showed good judgement and there was always a fair turn out on one of his theme nights. He tapped an empty bottle of whisky so that it rang out and caught his customers attention.

'Right then let's 'ave the best of order. I want you to give a sizzling welcome to Sir Lancelot Walters Wynn…storyteller, rhymester and quidnunc. That's a newsmonger to you lot.'

A distinctive character in a top hat, riding boots and a short horse whip took to the stage. His sunken cheekbones, translucent skin and penetrating orbs framed with black eyeliner were macabre enough but his threatening delivery of speech brought an instant hush to the pub.

'I'm going to make your flesh creep.'

He adopted a thrusting posture that made some of the locals step backwards.

'Aha…my ability to disturb might just be based on the idea that what I say is true. As true as the night.'

The lights dimmed and the band exchanged mocking looks. The rhymester continued.

'I will mix you a strong brew of supernatural ideas and this evening I will drain thoughts from Mr Bram Stoker's Dracula.'

He moved off the stage and began to creep amongst the crowd. Cerys held onto Dylan as the storyteller moved closer. The performance continued.

'The tomb in the daytime when wreathed with fresh flowers had looked grim and gruesome enough, but now, some days afterwards when the flowers hung lank and dead, when the spider and the beetle had resumed their dominance, when rusted iron and tarnished brass gave back the feeble glimmer of a candle, the effect was more miserable and sordid than could ever be imagined.'

Dylan felt Cerys's body quiver.

'Cerys you're shaking like a leaf.' She looked up and whispered.

'Well how do you want me to shake?'

They chuckled and Dylan knocked back his drink. Sir Lancelot Walters Wynn slithered to the other side of the room

'The vampire hunter, Abraham Van Helsing, went about his work holding his candle so that he could read the coffin plates and gripping it so that the waxy sperm dropped in white patches which congealed as they touched the metal. He made assurance of Cerys's coffin then searched in his bag for his turnscrew.'

All the young friends looked at Cerys. Suddenly, Sir Lancelot was amongst them. He lowered his head and moved it around the group like a serpent.

'You think you baffle me, you with your pale faces all in a row, like sheep at the butcher's. You'll be sorry, each one of you. You think you have left me without a place to rest but my revenge prospers…I spread it over centuries. The girls that you love are mine already and through them you and others shall yet be mine. My creatures to do my bidding when I want to feed feed feed.'

Lancelot lowered himself over Cerys and brought his fingers close to her neck. Dylan was put out. After all Cerys was his girlfriend.

'Hey keep yer hands off pervert!'

Cerys felt a little threatened but did not want to ruin a fellow performer's act.

'Dylan…don't,' she hissed.

Lancelot tilted his head at an odd angle and stared at Dylan.

'Of all the griefs that harass the distressed sure the most bitter is a scornful jest. Fate never wounds more deep the generous heart than when a blockhead's insult points the dart.'

The pub crowd tittered nervously. Dylan was embarrassed and angry.

'Hey, who are you callin' a blockhead?'

He rose and tried to grab Lancelot but was pulled back by Sticky, who seemed unusually keen to restrain Dylan. Lancelot backed away and turned to his audience who clapped in his defence and jeered at his attacker.

Lancelot pointed up at the large wall clock which had Roman numerals. It was a cue for the landlord to secretly trigger a switch on a battery that sent the hour and minute hands to fast forward. The clock became a spiral.

The crowd were cheering the storyteller now. He had won them over. He carried on with his macabre parody until the pub's bell rang out. The clock had realigned itself. It was 10.20pm. Big Al stood up on his tiptoes behind the bar.

'Thank you, Sir Lancelot Walters Wynn for your ghoulish

gifts. It's last orders ladies and gentlemen. Oh and if anybody wants to buy some refrigerated badger steaks, monkey brains or a lamb shank it's all going at half price tonight.'

The band stepped out into the cold night air. Dylan was still annoyed.

'What a load of horse shit. He had you lot goin'as well. Don't know why you got in the way Sticky. I should 'av floored him'

Sticky stiffened.

'Yer right. He was just a gobshite quidnunc or somethin'. Didn't want us kicked out that's all'

Cerys was more subdued.

'Well he had me worried. 'Specially with all that Cerys and the coffin stuff.'

Brian agreed.

'That was really weird.'

As they neared their van, Dylan stopped. His mood seemed to have changed

'Tell you what, as it's such a lovely night, what with the cheesy moon and me feeling all romantic, let's take a short walk…through the graveyard.'

Brian groaned

'Haven't you had enough? I suppose you want your hair to stand on end before the night's over.'

'Oh…come on,' Dylan said impatiently. He was already making for the graveyard gate.

The others reluctantly followed. As they entered the graveyard they were being watched. In the Black Cat's changing room, Sir Lancelot was looking at the group through a tiny window. He turned and used a towel to wipe the make up from his face. Then he removed his top hat.

'Carry on my sweetie pies. You'll soon be lining up for my own waxy white stuff.'

It was Professor Vasseline. He was moonlighting.

Cerys's band drifted through the grassy walkways gazing at the sculpted angels, decorated slabs of stone and fancy railings that protected the bigger tombs. The moonlight picked up on the memorial surfaces and it was possible to make out some of the lesser worn epitaphs and symbols. Brian, the group's keyboard maestro and intellectual illuminated them.

'See the anchor carvings? Well they're an early Christian symbol for hope. You know holding on against the odds. Angels are obvious. They're the guides who lead the souls of the dead to paradise. That circle over there that's an unbroken line. That's the idea of eternity…or living forever to you lot.'

Cerys was fascinated

'Didn't know you were into religion Brian.'

'I'm not religious but this place is a great directory of talking stones.'

Sticky butted in. 'Talking stones? I've heard of talking fish but…'

Brian ignored him.

'It's a catalogue of past lives see. A letter of introduction to those buried here. Sort of an open air museum.'

'So what's that mean Brian?' asked Dylan

They stopped at a broken pillar.

'Well a pillar shows strength and the ability to carry on. A sculpted broken pillar like that one shows the loss of someone who was prepared to share life's load.'

"What like us roadies?" Sticky suggested. Brian carried on pretending not to hear.

'Hands…that's the sadness of parting or the prospect of a heavenly reunion.

Ivy represents friendships that cling so tightly that they...'

'Yeah, alright mate.' Dylan was jealous of Brian's expertise. They reached the outer edge of the graveyard and found a gap in the circular wall. Beyond them was the tangle of bushes and trees that surrounded the old mansion house ruin.

'Come on we can't stop now. This is the best bit.' Dylan stepped into the unkempt garden. The others followed slowly in single file.

A badger who had just found some juicy worms was disturbed by the approaching footsteps. He slipped behind a fallen slab of stone, leapt over a sunken mound and watched the intruders from a safe distance.

'Hey… look at that.' Cerys had caught sight of another grave. The railings around it were broken and a few branches littered the site.

'It's a family crypt,' said Brian.

They peered at the words on the stone that had tilted to a severe angle.

'Eh… that's not the bloke in the top hat is it?' Sticky was trying to be clever. Dylan seemed to agree.

'Best place for him if it is.'

Cerys read the stone's inscription

'Sir Lancelot Walters Wynn…Mighty Regent of the Night 1715 –1774.'

Sticky was impressed.

'Regent of the night! Bleedin' hell I bet he stayed out late.'

'Do you think he's related to the pub's storyteller?' Cerys was intrigued by the possibility. She felt a frisson of excitement that it might be true.

Dylan sneered back

'Yeh… I wouldn't be surprised. He was creeping round us like a python.'

Cerys leant over the sunken grave and scraped away some of the ivy and moss that had grown over it. There were some more words chiselled in the stone just above ground level. They were difficult to make out. Brian supplied a flame with his Zippo lighter. Cerys brushed away the debris and attempted to read the stone.

'I shall raise up the dead and they shall devour the living.'

'That's really scary guys.' said Cerys looking over her shoulder for comfort.

'There's more,' said Brian,

'I shall make the dead outnumber the living.'

He looked at the others. 'This Lancelot must have been stark raving evil!'

Sticky maintained a know-all attitude.

'Bet you he actually lives down there for real.'

Cerys decided it was all going too far.

'The only thing that lives down there now is the mole what hangs round in the hole. Lancelot's been down there two hundred years. Come on, it's getting cold.'

Sticky felt he had a chance to impress his young friends.

'I reckon we should make sure Sir Lancelot doesn't pop out again.'

'Like how?' Dylan was still a bit put out.

'Like drive a stake through the ground to sort of pin him down permanently. Stop him annoying the ladies like.' Sticky was going too far. Cerys had had enough.

"Come on Dylan. Let's go."

Sticky tried to justify himself.

'No I mean it. We'd be doin' the peasants round here a favour.'

He walked up to a rickety wooden fence and ripped a piece off that had a pointy end. His friends groaned.

'It's a graveyard not a scrapyard ….you nutter.' Brian always knew Sticky was a bit of a liability. Even Dylan felt the same now.

'Time for me cocoa. See you later mate. Come on Cerys.'

Sticky carried on wrecking the fence. As the others walked back to the van Dylan called out.

'Hey Sticky…watch out for the bats. They've got big teeth round here.'

The trio walked back to the pub car park. Sticky would be alright. He only lived around the corner although they were not sure where exactly.

Sticky was on a mission He was in a dark zone, he was fixated on the prank. He looked around and picked up a large rough stone that had fallen off the circular wall. He threatened the grave.

'Regent of the night…prepare to meet your match.'

He knelt down and rammed the wooden stake into the uneven ground. Raising the stone he smashed it onto the blunt end of the wood. He pounded away at the stake driving it deeper into the ground. He took a sharp intake of breath as he thought he felt himself being pulled downwards. He stopped for a moment and looked around. There was no one else about. Sticky raised the stone and brought it down again. As he pounded the wood he felt himself being pulled down further towards the grave. Frightened now he began to hit the wood in panic. The harder he pounded the closer to the ground he was pulled.

'What the no…no!'

He attacked the wooden stake in a frenzy. With each successive strike he was pulled nearer to the grave. He had had enough. He tried to tear himself away.

'Ahhh you demon ahhhhhhhh…'

He stopped for a moment then began to cry.

'I submit to your power Sir Lancelot…please let me go,' he wept.

'I'll do anything for you Mighty Regent. I'll serve you. Just let me go. Let me go please please pleeeeeaaaassse.'

He tried to get up but he was held fast by the power of the grave. He cried pathetically and realised he was trapped.

'Dylan….Brian help me. Help me somebody…Cerys,' he pleaded but there was no reply. Then in a final burst of defiance he lifted the stone and hammered away like a mad fiend. As he was pulled down further his breathing became more erratic and he sobbed pathetically. He was succumbing to the dark horror below him. His hands were covered in blood from the rough stone and he was all but finished.

A boot suddenly appeared on the grave about an inch from Sticky's nose.

'Idiot! You're making enough noise to wake the dead!'

It was Professor Vasseline. Sticky was too far gone to speak. He mumbled and pointed at the gravestone. Vasseline bent down and whispered in his ear.

'You cretin. You've driven the stake through the bottom of your coat! Now get up before you feel the end of my boot where the moon don't shine.'

Sticky whimpered and tried to get up.

'Lets get out of here before we're seen fathead.'

EIGHT

A few days later the band were rehearsing a new song written by Cerys. They wanted to include it in a performance later that evening and needed to tighten it up a little more. Sticky had been watching the band's progress but he got bored. He went outside to prepare the van. He threw out some of the cartons and wrapping papers that littered the battered transit. As he tidied up the vehicle a headlight from an oncoming car slowly panned over his face. A sleek old Jaguar pulled up alongside the van and the driver's window slid down with a hiss. Sticky walked up to the Jag. A hand emerged holding a couple of jars. Sticky passed over some money and as he went to take the goods they were withdrawn.

'What's up?' protested Sticky. 'That's what I paid last time.'

A voice from inside spoke with dictatorial whine.

'You'll need to spread the stuff around a bit more if you want the price to stay firm. You're not buying enough Sticky. You've got to make the risk worth the trouble.'

Sticky tried to say something in his defence.

'I'll get some more orders! We're playing at a biker's wedding tonight. Should be good for a few extra orders and a new chain for my moped.'

The jars reappeared and he grabbed them just before the powerful car sped off almost taking Sticky with it as it disappeared into the night.

'Oi Sticky! Anytime mate.' It was Brian, who was often impatient.

Sticky turned and saw the band carrying some of their kit. The heavy stuff like the amps were still inside of course. Once

Sticky had humped the sound system out of the old workshop and placed it in the van he got in the front passenger seat. Cerys was in the so-called back seat which had been bolted in by their hard working roadie. It turned the old grocer's van into a vehicle more suitable for transporting musicians than sacks of cabbages. Still pleased with her newly acquired guitar, Cerys held it between her legs. Dylan snuggled in alongside and wrapped his arm around her. Brian and Sticky climbed in the front. Brian was driving.

'Do ya know how to get there?' asked Sticky. Brian grinned, revved up the old van mischievously and drove off erratically.

'I'm surprised you don't drive us in reverse seein' as you know the route backwards,' Sticky observed dryly as he passed some horseradish sauce over to Cerys and Dylan. The lovers dipped their fingers in the jar. After a minute or two Dylan felt light headed and began to tease the pusher.

'Hey, do you know, Sticky loves music so much that when he heard the Supremes were naked and singing in the bathroom he put his ear to the keyhole.'

Sticky put up two fingers. 'Av you bin looking in that old music encyclopaedia again?' he said as Brian swerved around a corner. Cerys jabbed Dylan in the ribs to shut him up but Sticky was up for the banter.

'If they gave you a dope test Dylan you'd get a bleedin' distinction.'

Brian blasted the van around another corner which made Dylan drop a large dollop of sauce onto his lap. He indicated at it to Cerys. She poked him in the ribs again and he doubled up with pretend pain. Up front Sticky was trying to piece together the remains of their map book while Brian looked on at his clumsy attempts.

'You know Sticky, one of these days we won't need to use

maps to find these venues. There'll be some sort of positioning system that'll enable us to follow a route on the dashboard.'

Sticky looked at him

'You're off your head you are Brian. Good job you've given the sauce a miss if you ask me.'

Dylan leaned forward and pulled a black curtain across the cab. He and Cerys had plenty of room on the rear seat. It had once adorned an elderly limousine. Dylan turned to Cerys and mouthed…*I wanna bite you.*

He put his hand behind her head and pulled her to his lips. She closed her eyes to better taste the moment. His mouth moved against hers and opened her lips wider. She felt very sensitive so that she could feel the lightest movement of his tongue. Cerys pressed her body against his and her breasts pushed against his chest. She wanted to wrap herself around him. She opened her mouth and pushed with her tongue. He moaned very quietly. Suddenly, they were thrown out of their embrace by the motion of the van. The swerving transit overtook a double decker bus that had just pulled up at a stop. A ticket conductor stepped on board the number twenty two and twitched a little as the band's transit van disappeared up the road. Van Hellbent Junior was having another one of his costumed turns. Something about the speeding van was disturbing the trance that had overcome him some minutes earlier. Dylan pulled back the drape to see what was going on. It wasn't great. He should have known with Brian behind the wheel. He was famous for his short fused driving technique. At a traffic light on a quiet road Brian jumped a red then quickly turned around to check his passengers were okay. Cerys was resting her chin on the guitar. As Brian turned back to face the windscreen he glanced up at his rear view mirror and saw Cerys apparently leaning on fresh air! Surprised and simultaneously trying to make a right turn, Brian was momentarily confused and was then faced with a car overtaking a slower moving vehicle in the on coming lane. Thrown into a panic he slammed on the brakes as the car just managed to squeeze by. All the passengers were thrown about. An amplifier perched directly behind Cerys shot forward and pushed her violently against the guitar's headstock. She felt a searing hot pain as it tore into her neck and filled her skull. The wire strings which were left loose at the ends licked her face and neck cleaning up the gore and liquids. The headstock itself had punched a hole in her throat and allowed the guitar body to suck up Cerys's life blood like a rapacious wolf. The instrument moaned excitedly and immediately appeared to glisten. As the band pulled up, Sticky thought the moaning sound was quite sensual.

'Got a funny squeal from the brakes there. Or was that you Dylan?'

Brian drove onto the verge alongside the road and pulled off behind some trees. More equipment crashed about. Sticky put his head in his hands. Brian turned in his seat and Sticky gave him a verbal lashing.

'Well you can say bollocks to tonight.'

Dylan was dazed but agreed.

'Bollocks to ton...'

'Hey! What's with Cerys?' cried Brian. They all looked at her and saw that her neck had been torn open and her head hung at an odd angle. She was lifeless. They scrambled out of the van. Dylan bit on his knuckles and had tears in his eyes. He was frightened and under the influence and started to back away. Sticky protested and was anxious about any dodgy evidence in the van.

'We can't just leave her here! We'll all be done!'

'Yes we can!' snapped Brian.

'But it was your fault. You were driving,' Dylan protested quietly and he had a point. Brian faltered.

'Er…well er lets make it look like she was drivin'.' He ran back to the van. Dylan sounded distraught.

'But she wasn't,' he sobbed.

'Yes she was,' countered Brian and he disappeared inside the transit.

Dylan looked at his watch.

'We're supposed to be on in a couple of hours. Are you sure Cerys can't make it?'

Brian carefully placed Cerys in the driving seat.

'I think she's got other plans mate.'

He manoeuvred around the body and accidentally released the handbrake with his knee. The van lurched forward and started to roll down a bank as Brian jumped clear.

'For Christ's sake stop the wagon!' yelled Sticky.

Dylan looked on helplessly.

'Oh…Cerys' I should've…'

The lads were too late to stop the vehicle moving but Sticky made an attempt at saving something. He was in and out of the van before it picked up speed and crashed through some bushes. He turned to his remaining band mates

'Okay then. We'll just say she was getting some fuel while we checked out the venue. Right… come on.'

You could rely on Sticky in an emergency.

The little group moved off and Sticky limped a little. Brian scratched his head.

'Weird how there was just a couple of drops of blood in the motor.'

Now that it was mentioned Sticky seemed to agree.

'Yeah maybe she felt sort of anaemic…and this is weird. It kinda looks brand new now.' He raised Cerys's guitar.

'What!' Dylan backed away from the glossy red guitar. Brian breathed fire

'You arse! That should've stayed in the van with all the other gear.' Sticky held the instrument close to his side.

'It's mine now boys. She owed me a few quid.'

They merged with the night.

The badgers couldn't believe it. No sooner had they fixed up a new home in a bushy back garden then a great heap of metal and tyres came crashing through their front door.

Van Hellbent Junior was first on the scene in his ticket collector's uniform. The number twenty two bus had a stop opposite the house where the transit van had ended up. Hellbent looked around the vehicle and examined Cerys. He noticed a distinctive mark on the side of her neck in the shape of a guitar. It was Fender Stratocaster-like with two small distinctive horns as cutaways. He drew a quick sketch and his attempt was partly illuminated by an incoming flashing blue light. A small crowd were gathering at the crash site.

'Right, who got here first? Did anybody see the accident take place?' Inspector Smollett looked around. Van Hellbent stepped forward.

'Inspector, I got here a few moments after the crash. There's something I'd like to show you.' Smollett screwed up his eyes and began to recognise Van Hellbent.

'Don't I know you from somewhere sir?'

'Yes, we met at the University. I was dressed....'

'That's right. I remember. You were dressed like a Monk.'

'Fakir actually...fourteenth century.'

'And what's the occasion tonight?' Smollett looked at Hellbent's uniform.

'Moonlighting on the buses are we? Don't the Government give you Professors a living wage anymore?'

Van Hellbent stammered in reply.

'I cccan't fully explain that yet…but I have found something. Look at this.'

He pointed at Cerys's neck and the mark of the guitar.

'I'm not sure who the killer is but this suggests a devilish candidate.'

Smollett put his face up against Cerys's lifeless body.

'Well it's got a devil like shape but it could be an insect. One of them Staghorn beetle things. These rock musicians have got wild imaginations. It might even be a tattoo.'

Hellbent didn't want to sound superior but he spoke like a bored teacher explaining something simple to a dull boy.

'I think you'll find that it is blood Inspector.'

Smollett rose to his full height.

'You seem very certain Professor. Now what were you doing tonight did you say?'

NINE

Apart from junk shops, Wrexford was endowed with a music super store that was as good as any in the country. Most of the stock was new but there were a few second hand electric guitars on offer and anything that looked like a Fender was welcome. Sticky emerged from Guitar City still limping but with a wad of notes in his hand. Behind him a salesman was already placing Cerys's guitar in the used section of the window.

Sticky was heading towards a four star hotel. He had received a phone call from a tour manager offering him a job with a sensational new band. They had an American front man who looked and played like no other. This was exciting. So exciting that Sticky decided to spend some of the money he made with Cerys's guitar on a new look for himself. A radical hairstyle should do it. It would help him with the grieving process too. A fresh start would enable him to put the tragic events of the last few days behind him.

The police seemed to have bought the story about Cerys going off for petrol while the band sorted out their equipment. She had no licence, so probably lost control of the van, concluded the investigating officer.

Sticky was genuinely upset about Cerys. When Frankie had died it was a shame of course but there was an arrogance about the man that made it difficult to really like him. Cerys was a real loss though. She was kind, funny and talented. Sure she owed him a few quid but he was glad to help her out at the time. He was so upset the day after her death he polished off a whole jar of horseradish sauce on his own. It seemed to make things worse.

Chrome accessories, coloured bottles, ground glass shelves, boxing magazines and a leather strop for sharpening cut-throat razors were the essential props in a barber shop and this one had the lot. But it also had a good reputation. All the sharp guys came here. This was Hair Raid.

'How about if I shaved the back in a vee line and curved forward around one ear creating a whitewall effect then stepped my way to the…'

'Listen son if I wanted sculpture I'd visit a garden centre wouldn't I?'

Obviously not all the customers were style conscious. Sticky overheard the chit chat as he walked in and took a seat. He watched two barbers in their short white jackets. One was a little older than the other and by the sound of him he was the owner. The senior barber was trying to persuade a reluctant customer to trust his young hairdresser.

'He's an artist Bill. To him every hair's a brush stroke on canvas. Every cut a piece of design. You should be grateful Joe looks on yer balding 'ead as the Sistine Chapel.'

'Aye well, let's settle for a Methodist chapel, I can afford one of those,' replied a voice that could only come from the valleys to the south. The young barber tried his favourite chat up line as he moved in on the elderly customer.

'Where did you go for your holidays Mr Roberts?'

'We went to Turkey.'

'Oh Istanbul was it?'

'No, it were lovely.'

It wasn't long before the old customer was satisfied with his short back and sides and left. Joe dusted off the cushion on the swivelling Belmont chair and invited Sticky to take a seat.

'What can I do for you sir?' asked the young blade.

'I've been thinking about leaving the sides long and having it short on top.'

'Okay. I'll see what we can do.'

The hairdresser kneaded Sticky's hair and felt its weight. He ran his fingers through the strands and Sticky enjoyed the sensation. He decided he ought to find himself a girlfriend one day.

'Your hair's like buttered Yak wool.'

'Is that good?'

'It's naturally greasy. I'm going to wash it then see how it takes to a shape. You sure you want it short on top cos I could build up a towering matrix and fix it with super gel? I could make a division through the hair just above the temple but I'll also thin the sides vertically to suit the shape of your head and the roots need to be laid in their natural direction to reduce the volume.'

Sticky tried to get a word in but failed. What the hell. He decided to go for it. Super snips worked at a pace but like most hairdressers he chatted up the customer as he worked.

'So, you in the music biz?'

'Yeah, I'm a roadie with a new act. Gonna be big. Bigger than the Stones or Gary Glitter. Maybe even Elvis.'

'No, really. Wow. Now early Elvis had a great look. He used to have that brilliant quiff didn't he. It was like a vinyl wave combed into a ducks arse round the back of the neck.'

'Hey pal this is nineteen seventy four not fifty four!'

'Yeah well hair's your crowning glory. You can become anybody with the right style.'

That was why Sticky came in. He was going to get his money's worth here. As Joe snipped away Sticky thought he'd catch out the expert.

'Okay maestro what's with the guys in monasteries? Why do they shave their skulls?'

'Monks are supposed to leave girls and that kinda stuff alone right. So maybe it's a form of castration.'

48

Sticky didn't like the sound of that.

'Okay, here's another. Why did American Mohican tribes shave the side of their heads but leave the middle bit standing up?'

'Easy. Those warriors wore their hair in a high crest to represent a continuous line of buffalos outlined against a flat prairie.'

Joe was waving his comb and scissors about as he answered the questions.

Sticky looked up at the young barber.

'I reckon they did it to look cool and scare the shit out of the white man.'

'Let's try something else,' said Joe.

TEN

A newspaper headline with giant letters shouted out 'ANGLO AMERICAN SUPER GROUP ON UK TOUR.' It was being read by someone with shaky hands. Van Hellbent Junior, dressed as a porter, was nervously scanning his paper in a hotel foyer. **THUMP** he was jostled to one side. The hotel became a flurry of activity as three rather grand rock musicians passed through the lobby. One of them possessed a garden shed sized hairdo. A reporter and his posse ran up and attempted an interview.

'Mister Bendix are you and the Extensions religious?'

The rock god replied.

'All left handed musicians have much to be grateful for. We thank the Lord for our gift.'

The three musicians entered a lift and as the doors closed a spokesman made an announcement.

'The Johnny Bendix Extension will be playing extra dates on this tour. I have the details right here folks.'

An asylum of rock journalists crowded around the man with the info.

In a hotel suite high up in the marble and glass palace, Johnny Bendix sat on the edge of his bed holding a sunburst guitar which he strummed gently. He drank some Hungarian Bulls Blood wine then strummed some more. There was a knock at the door.

'It's Harvey here.'

Johnny mumbled a reply. 'Uh...yeah.'

The door opened and a shiny suit walked in. Harvey had the aura of a Mr Big and enjoyed playing the part. He was the band's manager. He was as wide as he was tall and wore black patent leather shoes.

'I've brought the new roadie up to help get your stuff ready for tonight. OK?'

Johnny seemed at ease.

'I guess...what's his name?'

'Sticky. Just Sticky. In you go boy.' Harvey pulled Sticky forward.

Sticky got what he had asked for. A bouffant mullet hairdo that looked as though it had been styled with a whisk. Harvey shrugged his shoulders and started to leave.

'See you later Johnny…and don't take too much of that bull's liquor shit now. We need you on form tonight. All the music journos will be out there in the theatre looking for blood. You know what I mean... tour just startin' and all.'

Johnny sat up.

'Well they're gonna get it. I'm gonna rip their guts out on stage.'

'Attaboy Johnny. See ya later.'

Harvey pirouetted on his patent leather shoe and waltzed off in the direction of the corridor. Sticky walked over to the small portable amp Johnny had in his room. He was nervous and still limped a little. Johnny was intrigued by this stranger.

'You can pick that up later Sticky. Hell, why do they call you Sticky?'

'Cos my surname is Glue.'

'Jeez, I thought you had a wooden leg or somethin'. You know like a false limb.'

Johnny knocked back another glass of the dark red wine.

'Oh my leg… I tripped over a dodgy cable. I'm fine now.'

'Want some of this?' Johnny lifted up the bottle.

'I can't handle it Mr Bendix. Bulls Blood makes me shudder.'

Johnny laughed.

'It's supposed to man.'

Sticky gained in confidence. After all the rock god had offered him a drink.

He put his hand in his leather waistcoat.

'I can however recommend a gallipot of pure white horseradish sauce. It's been refined on the best allotments…if you know what I mean. I can see you enjoy a tipple Mr Bendix but this is the real skull attack.'

Johnny played his guitar tremulously.

Leaving his new master with the white sauce Sticky stepped out into the corridor. The carpet was thick and felt yieldingly luxurious underfoot and the walls were hung with Athena prints in expensive frames. Sticky had seen these art posters in glossy magazines lying about the hotel. They were ink drawings by Aubrey Beardsley, a late nineteenth century illustrator whose trademark style was to use large areas of black, leaving large areas blank. The images were costume erotic from the art nouveau period. Sticky had glanced through some of the magazines in the antique lounge area while he was waiting for his new bosses to arrive. He remembered seeing a quote of Beardsley's which he thought peculiar at the time. *If I am not grotesque I am nothing.* It could be a rock slogan thought Sticky. This Beardsley could have done some great album covers. The roadie tracked past the pictures seeing his reflection in 'The Peacock Skirt', 'The Dancers Reward' and the one he'd seen everywhere, even in clothes shops, 'Isolde', which featured the lone figure of a tragic opera heroine drinking a love potion.

'She could be trying some of my special sauce,' mused Sticky as he reached his hotel door.

Inside room 546 Sticky walked up to his battered old suitcase. He hung up his two shirts, threw a couple of pairs of socks into a drawer and then he saw the reflection of his trousers in the wardrobe mirror. They had more wrinkles than a very dry prune. Sticky decided that in the present company, namely Harvey, he ought to raise his standards. He thought he would call room service but then his eye caught sight of an ironing board or something similar in the corner by the window. He tried to open it fully but it would not spread out. Perhaps there were some instructions somewhere on the device. Sticky turned the object around.

'Trouser Press,' he read. 'Electrically heated since 1963.' His eyes lit up. Perfect. Not that he'd ever used one but he had heard of them thanks to the Bonzo Dog Doo Dah Band who had sung about such contraptions. Their lyrics had satirised the trouser press and referred to it as an emblem of the middle classes. Sticky was no sociologist. He decided he needed trousers with creases that could slice bread.

'Let's do the Trouser Press Boogie,' he chirped as he pulled out the press as far as the electric cable would stretch and switched it on. Perhaps he could save some precious seconds by not actually taking his trousers off. Why didn't the manufacturers think of things like that? After all time was pressing too. He smirked at the thought.

Sticky forced the two boards of the trouser press as far apart as he dared. Then he inserted his right leg between them. He pushed the outer sides inwards and with a snappy clunk the press locked into position. Within seconds of attaching himself to the press Sticky heard a ringing noise. Could it be the temperature control? Maybe it was time to switch legs? As he considered how he should make the change the ringing got louder. Hell's teeth it was the telephone. Sticky grabbed hold of the press and tried to pull the sides apart. It was stuck. It was also getting rather warm in there. He tried again but no matter how hard he pulled the trouser press's jaws would not open. He peg-legged his way to the mains plug and tried to bend down. It was only possible by cocking out his pressed and now rather heavy leg like a urinating dog. Sticky pulled out the plug and turned to the telephone which was on the other side of the room.

'Oh shit!' Sticky clattered his way across the carpet and picked up the receiver.

'Sticky, it's Harvey. Listen kid I wanna go over to the theatre ahead of the schedule. I've got a few things to iron out over there and I figure you could drive me over in the truck.'

'Eh well er. It's a bit difficult at the moment I'm er…'

'Good. I'll see you in reception in two minutes sharp!'

Harvey put the phone down.

Sticky looked at his sandwiched and now withering leg. How on earth did he get into this jam? He stood up and fell over straight away. As he attempted to get up his trapped leg caught the standard lamp and it came crashing down on top of him. Sticky caught hold of the bathroom door frame and hauled himself up. He shook away the lamp stand and threw off the lampshade which had settled on his head like a sombrero. His hair was ruined. He was panting now and getting angry with himself. He turned to the wall and started batting and thrashing it sideways with his trapped leg. Somehow he was determined to smash that press.

Harvey meanwhile had left his room and had gone downstairs in the lift. He was looking at his watch. If this Sticky was any good he would already be in reception waiting for him. Sticky dragged himself across the floor as if he was trapped inside the jaws of an alligator. Jeez these things were heavy. Harvey got to the ground floor and looked around. No Sticky. He walked across the foyer. Maybe Sticky was already waiting by the truck. Sticky had got as far as the lift but it went down a fraction of a second before he had a chance to hit the button. Damn! He hobbled to the staircase and looked a long way down. The only way he was going to get to Harvey on time was to slide down the banister. As Harvey got to the swing doors he was met by a music journalist who wanted to ask him a couple of questions. Harvey was always good with the press. He enjoyed being the centre of attention and this was his way of grabbing a bit of the limelight. He stepped back inside the hotel for a minute. Sticky was sliding more quickly and more roughly than he had hoped. As he whooshed down his trouser press bounced on each of the steps jerking him off his perch. He was being shaken quite badly but hung on grimly.

Harvey had just finished talking to the reporter from New Musical Express and was leaving through the swing doors when Sticky came crashing through into reception. Seeing Harvey crossing the car park he speeded up and gave chase across the lobby.

Arriving at the truck Harvey was rather irritated that Sticky was not around. The roadie had plenty of time to get down here. He turned back to the hotel entrance and roared out.

'Oh my God! Watch those doors!'

Sticky was jammed in the swing doors and being tortured by the trouser press as guests tried to push their way in. They were oblivious to the leg snapping potential and Sticky's pain. Upstairs in his room Johnny Bendix was curling his hair with a pair of massive electric tongs when he heard a commotion outside. He walked over to an ornately framed window. He looked out and immediately below his room he could see the fire brigade involved in some kind of struggle near the entrance. Harvey was standing a few feet away with his head in his hands.

ELEVEN

Neon lights outside a theatre venue gave the civic building a West End feel. A colourful sign blasted out the words - TONIGHT THE NUMBER ONE SMASH. THE JOHNNY BENDIX EXTENSION. Inside the Grande Theatre the crowd were taking their seats. Harvey, the band's manager walked on the stage and waited until there was a hush of sorts. It was a sit down concert and he waved his arms around to steady the crowd before he announced the act they were all dying to see.

'Ladies and gentlemen, boys and girls and other mammals let's hear you all put your hands together for The Johnny Bendix Exxxtennnnshun!'

The curtain went up and the crowd roared with excitement. The rhythm section provided the heart pumping beat and Johnny the guitar fireworks. He gave them string bending pulls, hammered the frets, swelled up his amp and threw in some double stops where he played two notes at the same time. He delivered rapid clean runs and wailing solos. Then he played his guitar between his legs and pirouetted to the delight of everyone but in particular to Sticky who watched from the wings in adoration.

After the concert there was a horseradish orgy in the dressing room. Despite his watering eyes, a sure sign that he had overdosed on the sauce, Sticky began to haul the bands gear out of the theatre. As he dragged some cases out into a corridor Johnny called him.

'Hey Sticky…how's that leg?'
'Wrinkle free,' said Sticky
'Man what were you thinking?'

'I wasn't.'

'You said it. Now listen I'm running out of your saucy sauce. You've got to get me some more of the stuff. It sort of makes the stage a happy home… know what I mean?'

'Sure thing Mr Bendix. I'll stock up your fridge later on tonight. Er will you be paying up front like?'

Johnny stuffed a bunch of notes into Sticky's waistcoat pocket.

As Sticky loaded up the tour bus he decided to re-arrange some items. He pulled out Johnny's sunburst guitar and placed it against the wall. Then he stacked the amps to create more room at the back. Having done that he looked around outside the bus. It was dark, he wanted a pee and he was alone. He went to the corner of the building and started to relieve himself. Over by the guitar an arm appeared bearing an anchor tattoo with the legend…*Johnny Forever,* written across it. The hand lifted the guitar and left a space by the wall. Sticky was thunderstruck when he returned. He looked up and down the side street. There was no sign of anyone or the precious guitar but there was a telephone kiosk on the corner.

Sticky dialled a number he knew off by heart. He listened to the dialling tone then he heard a click as the phone was answered. Sticky pushed the necessary button and spoke into the receiver. It was a bad line.

'It's me.'

'Who?'

'Sticky.'

'Sicky?'

'No…Sticky.'

'Nasty key??'

'NO STICKY!'

'What do you want?'

'This is the big one. An important order. I can't let my man down. You've got to get me a dozen jars at least. One day we'll have the whole music biz sucking on this stuff.'

'Good man. Good man that's what we like to hear. Turn up at the usual place in an hour. I'll have your sauce.'

Down the motor city alleyway where the Cerys Clark Three used to rehearse, Sticky paced about in the chill of the night. He pushed his back against the grimy walls to stay out of the cold breeze. Then he saw the lights from the Jaguar.

'Get in the front.' The voice was commanding.

Sticky did as he was told then he nervously turned in his seat to face a shadowy figure.

'Have you got the stuff like?'

'Have you got the money... like?'

The driver's face was barely visible. Sticky handed over his wad. The man turned around slowly and counted out the money. It was Professor Vasseline who always felt inspired when he held cash.

'Rich the treasure sweet the pleasure and you can always double your money by folding it in half.'

Vasseline was involved in difficult horseradish research and if he could not get the grants he needed to further his investigations then he would have to take matters into his own hands. The black market was a way of keeping his lab going and it paid for a good night out. He handed over a carrier bag. Sticky got out and then watched the old Jaguar pull away into the darkness. He just knew that one day he'd have to penetrate Vasseline's inner sanctum.

TWELVE

The next day Sticky was in the rock god's hotel room and walked backwards as an angry oncoming beast called Johnny moved towards him.

'I've a good mind to smear your balls with this. Do you realise what that guitar meant to me. You piece of dung.'

Sticky tried to reason with Johnny.

'I only turned round for a second...'

Harvey who was looking on was not amused.

'Look kid, Johnny aint feeling too good so I don't care what it takes but I want to see a damn good guitar back in this room by the afternoon or I'll personally hold you out of the window by your ears...and that's if I'm in a good mood.'

Johnny threw an empty jar at Sticky who ducked and ran for the door. Harvey grabbed Sticky and slammed him against the wall.

'And there ain't no hiding place kid. So don't try nothin' funny cos we know everybody.'

Sticky pleaded poverty.

'I'm er a bit short of beans this week sir.'

With a familiar sigh Harvey pulled out some bank notes.

'You can work it off during the tour. And we're watching you. Do ya understand?'

Sticky tried to nod despite the grip exerted by Harvey. Something caught his eye and he turned away as another jar hurtled towards him. It hit Harvey on the back of the head.

Sticky walked along a sunlit street until he reached the Guitar City store where he had previously sold Cerys's guitar.

That guitar was no longer in the window. Sticky sighed with disappointment. He was fed up but went inside anyway. If he could buy a good second hand guitar he might still make a couple of quid on the deal. As he entered he heard a yelp in the back of the shop and Cerys's guitar landed at his feet. A pair of Doc Martens ran past the instrument. Sticky picked it up and noticed a drop of blood on the strings. He had a momentary flashback to the night in the transit van and choked a little. A little later Sticky entered the hotel lift. He hit the elevator button and counted the money he had saved and stuffed it into his jeans.

Johnny opened up the guitar case.

'Pinky...it's kind of a girl's colour.'

Sticky tried to sound like an expert.

'It's a kind of red really. A special edition paint job.'

'You don't say.' That seemed to make a difference.

'I'll leave you to it then Mr Bendix.'

Sticky started to leave. He felt he might just have got away with it. As he passed the bedside cabinet he placed two jars of the white stuff by a box of tissues and left. Johnny picked up the guitar and sat on the edge of the bed. He picked up an empty jar and started to play slide style. He amused himself with a Hawaiian melody but the jar immediately started to resist the movement of Johnny's hand. He started to feel his shoulders tighten as the guitar seemed to want to lift off from his knees. Wow...the white stuff really worked. Johnny wasn't sure if he was imagining things or if indeed the guitar was moving up towards his face.

Downstairs in the hotel foyer, Van Hellbent Junior was propping up a desk. He was dressed as a hotel porter and looked glazed. Two of the Extension walked past him towards their tour bus escorted by large men wearing black leather sport jackets. The hotel receptionist, a slick sharp suited character clicked his fingers at the porter and pointed to the rock band's boxes and cases. Van Hellbent turned around and approached the band's equipment as if it were material from outer space. He picked up a guitar case and examined it.

'Nobody touches the guitars except me pal.'

Sticky was in an uncompromising mood.

'Er..Just trying to be helpful sir' said a still vague Van Hellbent.

'Well shift those amps and reverb units then.'

A block of Marshall amplifier stacks started wobbling towards the exit as Van Hellbent wrestled with his load. When he attempted to negotiate the side doors Johnny Bendix came alongside. Unusually, he was carrying his own guitar case. A strange but satisfying moan seemed to come from within it. Van Hellbent looked around for the source of the odd but somehow familiar noise and accidently crushed Harvey, the band's manager, who was standing near the door.

That evening there was a lot of commotion outside the Grande Theatre. Lots of people had failed to get tickets for the second concert. The lucky ones were already inside and enjoying the music. The Extensions were on stage. Johnny started to play one of his wailing lead breaks. His amps were set on high gain and high treble and the amplifier feedback was being manipulated to breaking point. The more Johnny distorted his music the more frenzied his audience became. Then as tradition demanded it he flamboyantly indicated that he was about to show off some of his ultra tricky moves. Would he play behind his back or between his legs? Johnny had no choice. The guitar decided to force its way up independently and he had no alternative but to use his teeth as the guitar powered its way onto his face. Sticky was in the wings of the Grande's stage but it might as well have been heaven.

'OOooh look at that man. Only two or three others have done that before. Go Johnny go!'

Adoring newspapers, rave reviews and sell out concert posters were promoting Johnny like the new Messiah and his guitar sound and antics were becoming legendary. To look at him you would not believe it. Despite his success Johnny was looking pale and haggard. His appearance worried those closest to him and it worried his management even more. Harvey walked Johnny down the hotel corridor to the star's gloomy bedroom.

'Look kid don't blow it. You're bigger now. Absolutely huge. You're world class. Even Royalty and TV Quizmasters want to meet you. But you gotta leave this white stuff alone. It's killin' ya. Go back on the Bulls Blood…I can deal with wrecked hotel rooms. But this new stuff! Hell you're losin' weight. It's like you haven't slept all week. You're so thin and pale it makes me ill just to look at you. Tell you what Johnny, I'll buy you a liquor store one day just promise me you'll give up the horseradish sauce.'

Johnny tried to mumble. Harvey continued.

'Maybe we should ease up on the schedule. I'll look at next month and try and lose a few dates. What do ya say?'

Johnny nodded wearily as Harvey pushed him through his bedroom door.

A squad car passed by a parked milk float that had pulled up outside a police station. Inside the cop shop Inspector Smollett paced around an interview room. He had a troubled and confused expression on his face as he listened to a visitor.

'Perhaps something is falling into place. These clues are a message from a friendly power that is trying to help us,' said the visitor.

Smollett tried to work things out.

'Let's get this straight now. There have been two mysterious deaths and you say that a blood sucking creature or thing is responsible and that there may be a musical connection?'

'Yes... er would that be two pints of milk or three Inspector?'

'Is it full cream?.. What the...don't change the subject.'

The visitor was none other than Van Helbent Junior dressed as a milkman.

He began to feel rather strange.

'Ooooh I think I'm getting a feeling...'

'Not on my carpet you don't.'

'No no. I'm sure the evil thing has visited again. I have this tingling sensation whenever it happens.'

Smollett raised his eyebrows.

'Tingling! The only thing that's gonna tingle around here are my cell keys when I lock you up for wasting my time again.'

The phone rang. Smollett answered it.

'Right. I'll be there straight away.'

On the other side of town Johnny Bendix lay in a crumpled heap on his bed. Harvey was visibly upset.

'I told him time and time again. But he wouldn't listen.'

He picked up a jar of horseradish sauce and as he examined it Inspector Smollett took it off him. Other policemen milled around. Smollett sniffed the contents of the jar.

'I'm reliably informed that this makes vindaloo curry seem like mother's milk sir. It's not to be trifled with.'

Johnny's body lay on the bed with the right side of his head uppermost. On the left side of his neck by the pillow there was a horned mark in the shape of a guitar. It was just discernable. Smollett shook his head and turned to Harvey.

'Terrible shame sir. Such a wonderul show biz career. Cut short by a heart attack I've just been told. Will you carry on?'

'The band will have no future without Jimmy,' sighed

Harvey, 'I'll just have to kiss the sky. Same as I did when his brother died four years ago.'

'Scuse me?' said Smollett.

THIRTEEN

Whitelock's auction house had been in business for over two hundred years. They had earned their reputation in Victorian art and Pre Raphaelite paintings in particular but had recently moved into pop and memorabilia. Rock 'n' roll was barely twenty years old so it was a brave move. A grand looking man in a bulging three piece suit and bow tie sat in the auctioneer's chair with his hammer in one hand. He brought it down in rapid succession as the various lots came and went. A pair of blue suede shoes, allegedly the ones that inspired Carl Perkins to write his hit song had gone for five hundred and fifty pounds. It was an astonishing amount. You could buy a brand new Mini car for that said a punter.

The auctioneer realised that a very special lot was coming up so he employed some theatrical emphasis in his pitch.

'Lot six six four is a purple and gold velvet jacket owned by the extraordinary and mercurial Johnny Bendix. The item was worn by him during his last performance. What am I bid for this unique costume. Who'll start me off at two hundred pounds?'

There was a hum amongst the bidders and the two assistants working the telephone kiosks kept a close eye on the action. The hammer eventually came down on four hundred and eighty pounds. The auctioneer moved on.

'Lot six six five is one of the stars of the sale this afternoon. Mister Bendix's very own guitar. A fretted maple neck with a tremolo and three pickups, the pickup at the bridge being angled and the whole on an alder wood body with the patina expected of a rock 'n' roll great. This will be an icon one day.'

A porter took out the guitar from its case and showed it off. The auctioneer continued.

'This is a once in a lifetime opportunity. Who'll start me off at one thousand pounds?'

There was nothing but a murmur. The auctioneer did his best and the guitar eventually made five hundred and thirty pounds.

'Sold to Mister Gordon Jones. I'm sure this guitar will be a worthy addition to a renowned collection. Right ladies and gentlemen, the one you've all been waiting for. Lot six six six is...'

Gordon, who had previously sacked his brother in law, Frankie, at the guitar factory, arrived home soon after making his winning bid. It was a flashy house and the interiors looked like ornate displays in an expensive department store. Gordon looked very pleased with himself as he carried an instrument case along the hallway. He stopped by a white console table to look at a large postcard leaning against the telephone. It had been put there by the cleaner. The card depicted a sunny Mediterranean scene with palm trees and fishing boats. He read the message.

'Still getting over Frankie's horrible accident. Decided to stay until the weekend. Love Moira.'

Gordon rubbed his thumb over her name affectionately and flicked the card back onto the table. He walked up a curved staircase and crossed the upper hallway into a long gallery.

The walls would not have disgraced a modern museum. The collection of rock iconography and guitars was matchless. Gordon was ahead of the game and he was sure that these investments would pay off handsomely one day. Along the black walls shiny brass name plates indicated the guitar greats that had owned each instrument on display. Pete Townshend, Duane Eddy, Buddy Holly, Scotty Moore, Chuck Berry, Ike

Turner, B.B. King, Eric Clapton, Dave Edmunds, Suzi Quatro, Keith Richards, Hank B. Marvin, Eddie Cochran, Jeff Beck, Jimmy Page, David Jon Gilmour, Bert Weedon and another Suzi Quatro…which was a Fender Precision bass. The other being a Gibson EB2. There were some missing guitar heroes but the collection was still growing. Gordon fondled his newest acquisition and removed it from its case.

'One more masterpiece. Ahh, to think that discount carpets, a little factory and a chain of chip shops have made me one of the world's premier collectors. Thank you God.'

He put a backing cassette into his hi-fi and attached a strap to his latest buy. As the music played Gordon joined in with a simple honky-tonk accompaniment. He postured ridiculously in front of a mirror.

'I play just like Johnny…I use both hands. Whaahaaaayyyy.'

Behind the high stone walls of the university, Bramble made his nightly tour of the quadrangle. He had just scraped off some dirt from one of his lamp-posts and given it a wipe so now everything was as it should be. Inside the west wing of the oldest part of the building, the part where the college dons had their oak panelled chambers, Van Hellbent Junior was frantically searching through a mass of books that sprawled all over his desk. He held a small sketch in his hand. It was the drawing he had made of the horned guitar mark on Cerys's neck the night of the road accident. He was trying to identify the mark using the books laid out before him. There were images of broken mirrors with different arrangements of cracks that had various meanings, there were rose flowers with odd thorns, goblets in the shape of monsters and even a section on alder trees that talked of their malign spirit. These trees appeared to bleed when cut and ancient burial places contained flints with alder leaf patterns on them. Gypsies thought it unlucky to pass such a tree whilst on a journey and looked the other way. Van Hellbent was particularly fascinated by a large scale drawing of an alder leaf. It revealed irregular teeth along the edge that were shaped like saw blades. Hellbent glanced over his shoulder and looked at four more piles of books. They reached from the floor right up to the ceiling. It was going to be a long night.

In another part of Wrexford, a caravan park illuminated by a neighbouring supermarket looked like a showroom for zombies. A block of brutal looking flats bordered one side of the old and decrepit site which gave the location about as much appeal as an upmarket shanty town. Sticky, who had lost his job after Johnny Bendix died, was looking for cheaper accommodation. He was being shown around the mobile homes by a large man dressed in a donkey jacket and battered trilby hat. The site was generally inhabited by migrant workers, so called missing persons and retired, delusional truck drivers, who thought they were cowboys. The site owner and Sticky stopped by a small yellow caravan. It was the smallest and scruffiest on the site. Sticky sighed.

'How much do you want for that?'

'Thirty quid a month. Payment in advance and you can do what you like in there. No questions asked.'

'Oh great. I can just see every sophisticated chick for miles around queuing up to shag the last of the big spenders in there.'

'Stranger things have happened. You never know mate.'

The site owner tried to sound optimistic then added.

'I expect you'll want a fart sack as well?'

About a hundred metres from the yellow caravan a male badger was examining a hole in the ground which had already been excavated by a previous generation of omnivores. With a bit of extra burrowing the passageways could be made habitable once again.

Not far away, Gordon strummed his guitar and strutted around his home museum like a fat duck. His stuck out his saggy bottom and wiggled it about. He took on an expression of theatrical intensity as he hit the strings then yelped. The guitar was having a quick drink. Gordon looked at his cut fingers and whipped off the guitar in pain and frustration. He walked over to an empty space on his gallery wall, slammed the guitar onto a couple of sprung loaded brackets and stood back sucking his fingers to relieve the stinging sensation.

'No doubt about it. What a mean guitar!'

A couple of streets from Gordon's home a chip shop was frying a new batch of crinkle cut potatoes. Alongside the counter there was a large picture of Gordon giving a thumbs up sign. At the bottom of the poster, 'Gordon's Salt n Battery', was spelt out in the colours of the Union Jack. A sleep walking Van Hellbent Junior was serving behind the counter. There were a couple of other night merchants in the back room sorting out a sack of spuds. The turn over of staff at the chippy was high so Hellbent's arrival caused no particular surprise. As Van Hellbent stared at the boiling froth of oil that the chips were being fried in a customer entered. It was Sticky.

'How much for a whopper sausage and jumbo sized fries?'

Van Hellbent looked at the hieroglyphics on the black board.

'Er... twenty and thirty, no twenty five pence, makes er nearly one pound er that's over forty pence mate er sir.'

Sticky counted out some loose change.

'Just the fries then.'

Van Hellbent threw the chips into a bag and Sticky left. Van Hellbent Junior stared after him. He knew that face from somewhere.

Gordon's guitar gallery was partly lit by moonlight. The horned guitar seemed to take strength from the moonbeams and began to pump slowly at first but with increasing exposure to the lunar light the pumping became more hurried. The guitar tried to push out against the wall brackets but they held firm. The guitar was thirsty. It had only taken a drop from Gordon and tonight it wanted more. A car pulled into the driveway outside. Its headlights flashed across the room and panned over Gordon's latest buy. The guitar wailed in torment.

Gordon parked his car around the back of the house then walked round to the front. He entered the hallway and tried to close the door with his foot but he was distracted by a strange noise and it was left ajar. His hands were covered in sticky plasters that he had just bought at the supermarket opposite the caravan site. As he removed his overcoat he heard a familiar sensuous wailing sound from upstairs. It was the kind of sound Moira made when she wanted to stroke him.

'Moira..!' he called. 'Is that you? Back already love?'

He smiled and trotted up the stairs. He would have to think of an explanation for his plaster covered fingers. This might not be the time for clumsiness he decided. The wailing drew him to his bedroom but when he looked inside he was disappointed to find it empty. The wailing got louder and Gordon realised it came from his guitar gallery. He stepped across the corridor and entered his rock museum. Perhaps he had left the jack plug in the guitar and if the amplifier was switched on it might be giving off some feedback. Gordon approached the horned instrument as it cried to him and put his head by its alder wood body to see if the jack plug had been left there. Immediately the tremolo arm sprang forward and clamped Gordon's head tightly to its wire strings. The metal cut into his face. His eyes rolled and he instinctively sensed the danger emanating from the guitar beast. He tried to shout out but only a muffled sob came from his body. He placed his large hands against the wall and tried to push himself free but it was as if he was held by some mighty constrictor which tightened its grip with each of Gordon's diminishing breaths. Blood started to run out of his ears and nose and he felt that his heart would explode. There was a sound like a drain sucking up great amounts of liquid and Gordon visibly shrank. His heart was denied its essence and it gave up the struggle.

A group of Japanese tourists keen to sample some ethnic cuisine had entered the chippy. They stood before Van Hellbent who called out to one of his back room boys.

'That'll be four Dragon burgers, five pickled eggs and some red sauce. If that's not too much trouble.'

One of the tourists took out a camera and took a flash photo of the chip shop. The burst of light brought Van Hellbent Junior to his senses and he realised he had strayed again.

Sticky was some way up an unfamiliar street and was prodding at his bag of chips. He was fed up. He added the remains of his horseradish to the fries but it had little effect on his mood. Moments later he passed a row of Edwardian villas. Large shiny cars lined the driveways. Sticky glanced at them and then he looked down at his bag of cooling chips and did a double take. A door was ajar in one of the houses. There was no car in the driveway either. It looked inviting and at that moment the street was empty. Sticky looked around and seeing the coast was clear stepped off the pavement and walked up the drive. It was shielded from its neighbours by a high laurel fence. On the other side of the street a curtain twitched.

Sticky looked over his shoulder again and sneaked up to the open door. He thought he might be able to grab a jacket or handbag in the hallway if he was lucky. Times were hard, life was tough and he needed to pay his rent. Sticky pushed open the door a little further. There was an overcoat lying by the phone on a small table. He stuffed his chip bag into his pocket. There was no noise coming from the ground floor. Perhaps the owner was upstairs. Sticky tiptoed through the hallway towards the coat. As he put his foot down on the carpet just in front of the table there was the burp sound from above. He stepped back outside quickly and peered through the crack in the door by the hinge but no one came downstairs. He waited a minute then decided to try his luck once more. He crept towards the coat grabbed it and rifled through the pockets as fast as he dared. They were empty except for some first aid sticking plasters. Sticky's heart sank. He decided to leave but just as he reached the door he heard a distinctive wail. Sticky froze.

Upstairs in the gallery the scene looked normal enough. Well apart from the expensive guitars hanging on the walls that is. A head poked around the door frame. Sticky stuck close to the wall as he slid round.

'Allo…anybody in…Allo? Pizza er chip delivery…'

He held onto his soggy bag of fries. He could always pretend he had got the address wrong if he was challenged. There was no response and Sticky feeling his luck was in stepped inside the room. He gawped at the collection.

'Shiiit'

He scanned the row of guitars and felt his pulse quicken.

'Whoa! It's jumbo sausages and pie tomorrow night…with gravvvvy.'

As he looked around the room the horned guitar made a sound like a breeze floating over its strings. It drew Sticky towards it and he noticed it was the only instrument without a wall plaque.

'Too valuable to identify eh?' he nodded to himself.

He had not recognised the horny instrument. Lots of rock acts had a red guitar in their line up. He had only to look around to confirm that but this was a bit special. He was mesmerised by the ultra glossy paint that saturated its body. Was that a twinkle? It was so richly coloured its allure was irresistible. Sticky leaned forward and tried to unclamp the reddest guitar in the world from the wall. It stuck firm then enticed him with a whisper of its strings and its hypnotic effect made him reach out again. He gave it a tug but it was no good. Sticky looked around to see what he could use to prize off the instrument with.

Van Hellbent Junior was walking up the street when a police car seemed to appear out of nowhere and shoot past him. He stopped to watch it tear up the road. It was moving quickly but there was no siren or blue light.

Sticky was illuminated by an open fridge in the kitchen. He drank some milk and stuffed some slices of ham into his mouth. In the corner of the kitchen he noticed a mop and bucket. He squeezed his groin. He needed the toilet.

Inspector Smollett was driving home and he had just driven past a chip shop when one of his squad cars shot past him in the opposite direction. He glanced up and saw it in his rear view mirror. It was not hanging about. He braked, spun his steering wheel around and gave chase.

Sticky walked out of the upstairs toilet with a mop in his hand. In his other hand he held an aerosol of men's eau de cologne and sprayed himself with it. He felt more fragrant than vagrant as he walked into the guitar gallery and approached the reddest guitar.

It was glistening in the moonlight. He sprayed himself once more and as he turned to place the aerosol on the table he came face to face with Gordon!! Sticky screamed in surprise then terror as Gordon's body fell towards him. He rolled with Gordon and hit the floor in panic and embarrassment.

'I didn't know it was your place Gordon. Honest I wouldn't...'

All of a sudden Sticky realised the body was stiff. Perhaps there was another intruder in the house. Thrashing about he struggled up and twirled his mop in case someone else jumped him. Seeing he was alone or as alone as anyone can be with a corpse lying next to them, Sticky knew he had to make himself scarce pronto. Gordon might have died of a brain haemorrhage or heart attack or something but Sticky wasn't going to hang around to find out. He turned to the horned guitar and started to lever it from the wall with the mop handle. The guitar seemed to purr as Sticky struggled with the devices that held it tight. With an almighty push from the mop the clamps gave way. Sticky grabbed his booty and ran downstairs. As he reached the hall a police car was just pulling up in the driveway. He dropped the mop and turned to run into the kitchen. Sticky unbolted the back door and ran out into the night grazing Gordon's car with the guitar.

Inspector Smollett pulled back a white sheet. Gordon lay under it looking as pale as his shroud. Smollett shook his head.

'This is another one of those slasher incidents. Sergeant! Send a car to the University immediately! I want Professor Van Hellbent Junior here as soon as possible.'

A young constable entered the gallery. Smollett was still bent over the body.

'We've caught a suspicious looking character outside sir.'

Smollett twitched excitedly.

'Right bring him in Constable Williams! Well done lad.'

As the suspect was brought into the room Smollett's nose wrinkled up.

'Phew…what's that smell? It's like fried batter and vinegar.'

Sticky bolted down a side street with his ill-gotten gain. The strap Gordon had used on the guitar was still attached but trailing behind him as he hurried along. Jet, a large lurcher dog, was out on his evening constitutional when the leather guitar strap shot past him. Good game thought Jet. The big dog ran after Sticky. He soon caught up and grabbed the leather strap with his lupine jaws. Sticky was pulled up short.

'It wasn't me officer. Honest.'

Sticky turned and looked for the police. When he saw Jet he looked for a handler. There wasn't one. Hang on. This was a lurcher, the sort of dog favoured by gypsies. He would fight it off.

'Hey ya crapping machine. Come on now. Gerroff.'

Back in Gordon's house, Inspector Smollett had his hand on his chin as he spoke to Van Hellbent quietly.

'Incredible, they'll be frying Mars bars and bananas next.'

'Almost finished in here Inspector,' called out one of the forensic team.

'Er quite. Er good. Now look…' he said scrutinising Van Hellbent.

'Gordon Jones was a self-made man.'

'What you mean like Frankenstein?' said the Professor.

'No..no! In business! Cheap carpets, instrument factory, fast food that sort of thing. He was worth a bit too.'

'So do you think it might have been a business rival or a burglar Inspector?'

'I'm not sure. Jones spent all his spare cash on rock memorabilia. His wounds are just like those on the other victims. I think we've got a serial killer here. Some mad man or mad woman with a grudge against the rock world…Look at this!'

He pointed to the bloody mark of a guitar on Gordon's neck. Van Hellbent looked closer.

'I've never seen anything quite like it before. Except on the other bodies. I'm convinced it's the work of a blood sucker but I haven't been able to identify this mark in my Vampire directories.'

He began to draw the mark. Smollett prodded Gordon's throat.

'Well, who ever it is must have a funny set of gnashers.

You could open beer bottles with a mouth like that. Maybe we should call in a dentist?'

Van Hellbent sketched at speed.

'Hang on. I'll draw his teeth first.'

In a back street Sticky was still involved in a tug of war with the snarling lurcher.

'Sharrup ya flea bag, It's a guitar strap not a beef steak ya crazy dog.'

Seeing the flash of blue lights in the distance and worried that the police would soon trawl the area, Sticky reluctantly gave up the struggle. He crept off into the night through a nearby caravan park. Jet immediately turned and took off with the strap in his jaws and the guitar clattered along behind him. The lurcher took a shortcut through a churchyard. As he lopped along, the guitar bounced off a couple of gravestones which temporarily dulled its killer instincts. These were further checked by the odd stone cross that got in the way of the bizarre convoy. A badger who had been digging up a few dead mice around the monuments managed to duck just as the wayward guitar flew by.

Outside a newly built detached house, surrounded by classical Roman figurines made of concrete and fairy lights draped along the roof, stood a middle aged blonde woman with a heavy gold necklace. This was Tanya de Villeneuve, a former rock queen. She was on the porch in her high-heeled thigh length boots.

'Jet…Jet boy. Come on in now baby. There's a good dog. Come on now Jet...Jet.'

The dog ran across the lawn with the guitar in tow.

Tanya stepped forward to meet the love of her life.

'Well...what you got there boy? This makes a change from the usual old shoes and chicken bones eh Jet? Good dog...

good dog. Mummy's got you some lovely dead cat paté inside. Cooome on'

While the lurcher gobbled down his supper Tanya fondled the bruised guitar. She could not resist trying it out. When she plugged it in and struck the strings the sound was uncanny. A commotion like no other came out of the gramophone amplifier. The guitar had a severe headache after its battering in the graveyard and wailed uncontrollably. Tanya was stunned by the effect. She tried a few more strums. It was unusual and spine tingling.

'This could be it!' thought Tanya. She picked up the phone.

'Gwenda, I want you and the girls round here tomorrow at ten o'clock sharp. Yep, in the morning. I think I've got it. The sound that'll restore, The Stilettos, to their rightful place in heavy metal's premier league. Oh and bring some fairy cakes.' She put the phone down.

Tanya was illuminated by a morning sun which made her words seem as though they were touched by some sort of divine power. Arranged around her were old band mates. Middle aged women who seemed to prefer domesticity to the rock stage judging by the clothes they wore. Tanya carried on.

'There's still a ton of fans out there that want The Stilettos to make a comeback. I want it to happen, you want it to happen, your bank managers want it to happen, the studio wants it to happen, even Jet wants it to happen.' She went on.

'Look until today we've been missing that vital ingredient.'

'Talent?' chipped in one of the women.

Tanya was not going to be diverted.

'Now come on Gwenda that's no way to talk. This band isn't just image you know. We're...er interesting. We've got each other and what with a few bone shaking riffs and a bit of extra promotion I think we can re-launch the band.'

'What with… a costume change?' said another of the women.

Tanya slowed down her delivery.

'No…a secret weapon. Try this for size lady.'

The last of the women got up and took the battered guitar. Tanya encouraged her.

'Go on Rosy. Try it.'

Rosy played a screeching chord that created a hurricane force in the room. It sent a shock wave through every woman's hairdo and smeared their lipstick.

'What the hell…?' Gwenda groaned as she pulled her hair back to reveal her face.

'Aint it great,' said Tanya, 'It's gonna go down in history as the psychic chord. It's a miracle.'

The Grande Theatre so recently the venue for Johnny Bendix and his band displayed a new billboard and posters. THE RETURN OF THE STILETTOS - IN COLOURED LEATHER. The group had been a one hit wonder then hit the skids after their rhythm guitarist swallowed someone else's bodily fluids and died. The publicity was not good. It was a mystery that the police declared was better left to scientific minds. Professor Vasseline had been involved in the investigation and though the case was inconclusive it had launched him into the world of gooey liquids. The case gave the Stilettos a certain notoriety which they still enjoyed.

Crowds poured in to the theatre to see the rejuvenated act and their skin tight costumes. Most of the outfits were actually biker kit sprayed with car aerosols. The leathers were hanging up in the dressing room and there was a bit of an atmosphere back stage. Gwenda, the drummer was the first to speak.

'We are not wearing biker gear. It's just so dated.'

Tanya tried to be reasonable.

'But it's what everybody wants to see. It's sexy and you know…dangerous. Come on.'

Rosy was not so sure.

'Gwenda's right. If this is a come back we 've got to be sort of now. A bit ironic maybe. You know expand people's minds.'

Tanya was sticking to her guns.

'You can slap a grenade in their ears if ya wanna do that. Or you can give 'em good old heavy duty rock. Throw in some skin tight leather and this great new guitar sound and they'll be gagging for more.'

She called out to an assistant in the corridor.

'Right bring it in now!'

The assistant wheeled in a black coffin shaped case with gothic brass handles and opened it up. Lying in state on a satin sheet was the horned guitar. Tanya moved towards it pushing the assistant to one side.

'Thanks Sticky.' She turned to her band looking pleased with herself.

'It hasn't half improved since I plonked it in there.'

Gwenda was still uneasy about the new image.

'Looks like something from a Dracula picture if you ask me.'

Tanya had heard enough. She was the band's leader after all.

'Well I'm not asking. I'm telling. Just get out there and suck 'em dry.'

The crowd roared with anticipation. They had seen the posters and the band looked sensational. The Stilettos were about to hit the stage for the first time in years. Tanya had brought along her lucky mascot, Jet. After all he had brought the band their new sound. He was parked backstage. She knelt down to give him a hug.

'You'll never have to eat tripe again my son.' She looked up.

'Neither will you Sticky.'

The band played brilliantly and looked like models from a

glamorous torture agency. Sticky was mesmerised. The fans were beside themselves. Even Brian, the keyboard player from the Cerys Clark Three was there. He was looking for a new band. Since Cerys's death things had gone from bad to worse. Dylan the drummer had become a recluse and Brian was keen to move on. Joining an all girl band was not really an option but he had to circulate and put himself about.

The concert sound seemed to carry on the air as far as the other side of town. It drifted through an open window at the university like a zephyr. Van Hellbent Junior could hear the music in the background but he was engrossed in his search for the elusive mark, the subtly horned one that the murder victims had on their necks. He had checked scores of books and papers but he had not yet found what he was looking for. As he turned to an old voodoo manual he flicked through the tannin coloured pages and found an image he needed to look at more closely. It was a picture of Mabon Du, the bat God and ruler of the underworld of Ogof Berwyn. Van Hellbent examined the picture with a magnifying glass. It was a close match and it had an attached story. It seemed that two musician brothers tried to defend themselves from killer bats in a dark cave in the Berwyn Mountains of North Wales. Soon they were forced to hide inside their flexible drums as they were being overwhelmed. After a few hours one of the brothers lifted his head up to see if the sun had risen and Mabon Du tore off his head and carried it away so that his fellow gods could use it in a ball game. Van Hellbent looked up. Now then, most of the Wrexford victims had their heads partly severed so this was worth a second squint. When Van Hellbent increased the magnification on his eye glass he noticed that the image in the book had tiny wings and a third horn.

'Voodoo shmoodoo. Voodoo you bloody well think you are Van Hellbent?'

The professor mocked himself and continued the search. Following this latest near miss the distant sound from the Stilettos began to annoy Van Hellbent. He needed to concentrate. He walked over to his window and tried to shut it but it was stuck. He stood there a while as the distant wail washed over him like autumn rain. After a few seconds Van Hellbent brought his hand down over his face. He was soaked. Just his luck to have a window stuck open on a wet night. He went off for a towel to hang over the gap. He would speak to Bramble about this in the morning.

At the Grande Theatre, The Stilettos became more and more confident. Rosy the lead guitarist had the horned guitar on her hip. As she leant forward into a string bending frenzy the large crucifix around her neck dangled over the guitar body. The horned one reacted with violent terror and went out of tune. The sound was horrific. The band became confused and the fans agitated. The ear splitting screech coming from the guitar was excruciating. Even when Tanya ran over to the amplifiers and pulled out the plugs the terrible deafening sound continued. There was no relief from the banshee like screams. The fans could endure it no more and bolted for the doors. The crazed guitar was thrown into its coffin like case but howled on and the distraught band abandoned the stage and ran out of the theatre. Jet was trampled by the back stage crew. Brian was badly crushed by the escaping horde and would spend the rest of his life in a wheelchair.

As Van Hellbent was fixing his towel to the curtain rail he was suddenly slapped up against the window frame. It was that something that should not be happening was about to happen moment. He felt dizzy and the ground below started to go out of focus.

The next morning as a street sweeping machine brushed up

outside the Grande Theatre a cleaning lady arrived at the stage door. When she entered the auditorium and saw the debris from the night before she muttered a few curses under her breath. Outside the theatre a sandwich board man with a, THE END OFTHE WORLD IS NIGH, message clattered about. He patrolled the pavement area directly in front of the Grande's main doors. Van Hellbent Junior felt uncomfortable but had yet to work out why.

The cleaning lady shuffled into the dressing room previously occupied by The Stilettos. She picked up some empty jars of white horseradish sauce.

'I don't know what the world is comin' to,' she moaned.

'Bloody musicians leavin' a mess like this…and the girls are worse than the boys.'

She picked up an old publicity shot of the Stilettos wearing skimpy studded bikinis.

'If God had wanted us to go around naked we would have been born that way…disgustin.'

She heard a pained wail and looked towards the open door.

'What's that …ello. Ello?'

She moved nearer to the door and noticed something behind it. The band appeared to have forgotten what looked like a black coffin shaped guitar case. The cleaner dragged it out into the middle of the floor.

'Fancy leavin' this behind. They ought to be charged storage. That'd wake 'em up a bit.'

She opened the case and stroked the guitar strings. She felt a tingle then picked up the guitar by its neck. It was surprisingly heavy.

'Ooooh you are a big boy!'

Van Hellbent froze as he heard the scream from inside the theatre. That was it! He was not meant to be outside walking about with a billboard around his shoulders. He was meant to be in the theatre. Van Hellbent ran up the stairs but his progress was hampered by the sandwich board as he reached the swing doors. The splintering of wood might have slowed down a lesser man but Van Hellbent Junior was trying to apprehend a killer. He had to find the source of the scream. A gurgle alerted him in the direction of the dressing room. He crashed along past the rows of dark red velour seats sending out more shards of timber and arrived inside the dressing room with the remains of the board still attached.

'Oh no!' He found a pitiful sight.

Police cars started arriving outside the Grande but Inspector Smollett was ahead of them. He was in the dressing room sniffing the remains inside some of the jars. He wanted to confirm his suspicions and he was right! It was that weird horseradish sauce. His forensic team meanwhile dusted the glistening guitar for evidence. Smollett snapped at them.

'Okay, take the banjo away once you've done the fingerprinting.' He was anxious to show some decisiveness. These gory crimes were getting to be an embarrassment. His manor was being stalked by some evil killer and he was getting nowhere fast. Van Hellbent was examining the dead woman's neck.

'This mark is the same one Inspector. Same as all the others.'

Smollett was all for taking action.

'Right, that's it. It's those high-heeled witches. Bring 'em in. I want the whole band arrested. All the victims have been topped in some sort of connection with the rock business but God knows why they would have taken out a granny like this. She's practically been eaten. That Horseradish stuff must drive 'em nuts.'

FOURTEEN

The Stilettos were milling about near the sergeant's desk. Their lawyer was on the phone booking a taxi. In his office, Inspector Smollett was worn out and wrung dry by the vampire-like crimes. He whinged to a couple of fellow detectives who noticed that their boss's fingers were covered in plasters. Smollett complained.

'Alibis...everybody's got a bloody alibi. What's worse is they all check out. And that blonde bomb crater, Tanya de Villenieuve, Tanya the villain more like. She says her dog is in traction! Where's it gonna end. I can't take much more of this.'

Down in the cells, Constable Williams delivered a tray of tea and sandwiches to a prisoner who had been arrested for disorderly behaviour. The inmate was a dishevelled man with a tattoo of a bat on his neck. He called it his guardian of the night. When the man turned around Constable Williams was thrilled.

'Blimey, aren't you Keef Pritchard of the Bones. I've got all your audio cassettes. You're my all time favourite. Can I trouble you for an autograph sir?'

Keef stirred a little.

'How do I know you won't use it in a bent confession?'

He sipped his tea while P.C. Williams was lost for words.

'Er..'

'Just kiddin' kiddio,'

Keef scribbled his signature on a charge sheet. The sound of a badly played guitar leaked into the cell. Keef looked up at the young constable.

'Have you added something to my beggars banquet? What the fuck is that?'

Williams gathered himself.

'Oh that'll be Inspector Smollett, mister Pritchard. I think he's a frustrated Country and Western artist. Ever since we brought a red guitar in as evidence he hasn't been able to resist the odd twang.'

Smollett's hands were covered in blood. His colleagues rushed up to him and bundled him out of his office towards a washroom. Smollett protested.

'But I only twanged it a couple of times...'

One of the policemen whispered to his sergeant.

'Sarge...whether he likes it or not I think he's going to have to go on sick leave. All we've got is another entry in the catalogue of mysterious murders. We're at a dead end and Inspector Smollett needs to rest. He's not been the same since this rock 'n' roll caper. Apart from which if I hear his guitar boogie shuffle once more I'll eat me own truncheon.'

The sergeant tensed up but nodded conspiratorially.

Inside his university chambers, Van Hellbent Junior put his last big tome to one side. It joined a monster stack of books that took up most of the space in his room and spilled out into the corridor. He considered his next move.

'That's it, no more references. I've exhausted every known fact, entry and word on vampires and the un-dead. I vowed never to seek help from the family but I admit I'm beat.' He looked heavenward.

'Great great Uncle Augustus, its time to climb the ancestral tree and sample the vodka berries. Saint Petersburg here I come.'

In the police cell, Keef Pritchard looked up from his bunk bed.

'Well, PC Williams what can I do you for?'

The young constable stood in the doorway.

'Seems a shame to let a good guitar go to waste. I thought you could do with this.'

He reached out into the corridor and brought out the horned guitar and presented it to his hero. Pritchard sat up.

'Did you know I was a musical prodigy? When I was five I wrote my first song. When I was six I made my first album. At seven I wrote a complete rock opera and at seven thirty I normally have a snort of the white stuff. Don't suppose you got any?'

P.C. Williams looked awkward.

'Just jokin' son.'

FIFTEEN

Behind the university were some mews cottages occupied by those of the academic staff who preferred to live outside the campus. Most of these former coach houses still had a garage or workshop where carriages used to be kept. Professor Vasseline had his private lab in one of these buildings. He was busy mixing up the raw ingredients that were the basis of his secret project. He was the Horseradish King.

Vasseline had perfected a sauce potent and addictive enough to stand alongside any recreational drug out there but the vital thing was that it was a native product. It was grown widely and available as an autumn crop. Vasseline's work was originally dedicated to the cure of in-growing toenails and the powerful sauce was a by-product. His formula was habit forming and for that reason had never been approved by the Medicines Control Agency. Horseradish mixed with vinegar and cream was used as a meat relish but Vasseline mixed it with other secret ingredients to create a hellish cocktail. It was more easily absorbed by the body and was easier to take than other substances and it had a growing number of users. Foiled by the Control Agency, Vasseline was not going to throw away his years of research. If he could profit by his version of the Horseradish sauce then that would compensate for the lack of honours coming his way. He felt particularly aggrieved that young professors like Van Hellbent Junior were celebrated for their successes but that he was mouldering away in comparative obscurity.

There was a knock at his garage doors and Vasseline froze. The only visitors he had were invited. As he never asked anyone around this was a surprise. He threw a sheet over his apparatus and walked to the double doors.

'Who is it?' he hissed anxiously

'It's me. Your cousin. Open up I'm freezing.'

Vasseline unbolted one of the doors and opened it a few inches. He stuck his head out and peered up the cobbled lane. His caller was alone and there was no one to see him enter.

'Alright, but get in quick. You know I don't like visitors here. What do you want?'

Sticky was glad to get in out of the cold.

'I've lost my last job after a riot at the Grande. There was a murder too. So the rock scene in this town is in a mess. I'm skint, starving and I've got no one else to turn to. You gotta help me. I need a job of some sort.'

Professor Vasseline looked at him. Cousins they might be but Sticky was a social embarrassment and an intellectual inferior.

'I've got nothing for you Sticky. My university work requires scientific knowledge and the sauce business is a secret formula. I couldn't possibly share it.'

Sticky was downcast.

'You don't care a fiddler's fart for me. You never have.'

'When we were at school who was good at chemistry?'

'Er..Guy Fawkes?'

'I know it was a long time ago cork brain but try again. Who?'

Sticky had another go.

'Er Einstein?'

'He was a physicist bird brain. Nooo it was me. I was good at chemistry and everything I was good at you were hopeless at. You were so lazy you wouldn't work in an iron lung. How you and I can claim to come from the same gene bank never ceases to amaze me. I suspect you were short changed by some biological cashier with a grudge against your parents. You've got what you deserve. All I can do is put you on my list of dealers. Take it or leave it.'

'But I'm already on your list.'

'Then you're in luck.'

SIXTEEN

Van Hellbent Junior walked along the banks of the river Neva. It was ten o' clock in the morning but the light was still poor. He'd forgotten what it was like in northern Russia. He should have put on an extra layer of clothing against the cold too. He lowered his head and walked past St. Petersburg's Winter Palace. As he crossed the great courtyard of the Tsars he was filled with a sense of pageantry. Imperial and Revolutionary forces had played out powerful dramas all around him. The city had been renamed Leningrad but the Hellbents always called it by its old name. The place made him tingle with emotion. Maybe it was being close to his ancestors or maybe it was just the ferocious cold.

Van Hellbent turned down a flagstoned side street with grand houses that hadn't seen a lick of paint in fifty years or more. Despite the surface decay these were still very fine homes and in one of them Van Hellbent would find his oldest living relative. He walked past windows and doors that were surrounded by carved stone and ornate wood patterns relieved by delicate metalwork. When he found the most imposing entrance in the street he knew he had found the house he was looking for. He pushed open the heavy wooden double doors and walked up a staircase that would not have disgraced an embassy. In socialist Russia each floor now housed a couple of families but there was a time when the Van Hellbents owned the property outright. The Hellbents though were always able to pull a few strings whichever power was in occupation. Tsars or Commissars they knew how to charm them all. This was the Van Hellbents

Russian branch and great Aunt Olga had the second floor all to herself.

Van Hellbent Junior entered an apartment that had barely altered since the turn of the twentieth century. It was ornate. Tapestries, rugs, painted portraits, a chandelier, deep buttoned leather sofas and other heavy furniture made the place look like time had stood still. It was a capsule from the family's past and Van Hellbent thought it magical. How it survived the Red Revolution and the sieges of World War Two he had no idea but it was here and it was fantastic. His old aunt rushed to embrace him. Van Hellbent recognised her scent. It was four-seven eleven, the original cologne and still popular with a certain generation. Olga wore an old fox fur stole over her shoulder and still used a lot of make up. She was excited by his visit.

'Ah my dear great leettle nephew. Dank you for your letters. Plis have some walnut vodka. It will warm you after ze cold outside.'

Van Hellbent Junior savoured the intense nutty drink. It was smooth and warming with a hint of treacle. He downed it in one. Olga knew he was on business and she had prepared everything. The Van Hellbents did not mess around when it came to the family trade.

'You are velcome to browse through ze notes my father, your great great uncle made in his investigations of vampires and ze undead.'

'Thank you great aunt.'

Olga went to a bookcase. Van Hellbent followed her but when he reached the bookcase he realised it did not exist. It was a tromp-l'oeil; a trick of the eye painting on a flat wall that depicted books on a shelf. The imagery was totally realistic. The painting was actually on the back of a flush door which great aunt Olga slid open. She revealed a great library that seemed to go on as far as Van Hellbent could see. Olga knew the enormity of the task ahead.

'Hard vork never hurt anyone who used somebody else to do it. Shame you are on your own my dear von. I would help but I must check on our beetroot harvest.'

Van Hellbent Junior was resigned to his fate.

'Yes well, I'm definitely my own researcher on this one aunt.'

'Good luck...I will leave you ze walnut vodka?'

Van Hellbent knuckled down to his task. He soon found links to fang land and all the areas that he needed to check on. He even came across a central European reference to alder trees and their malign spirits again. This case involved a peasant boy who had climbed into a tree. Soon after, four sorcerers dragged the body of a dead woman under the branches. They started to pull her apart and throw pieces of flesh up into the air. The young boy caught a piece of the woman and held onto it. When the sorcerers tried to rebuild the body they found they were a piece short so they made one to fit from the alder wood. The evil spirit that resided in the tree took over the revived woman and she brought famine and war to the area.

'Fascinating...but probably irrelevant. Now let's see what we've got under vampires,' Van Hellbent muttered to himself.

Over two thousand miles away, in a police station on the Welsh border, a police sergeant was releasing a prisoner from the cells. Keef Pritchard was about to see the Wrexford sky again. The desk sergeant was handing over his personal items.

'So...you got away with it this time but we'll keep an eye on you Mr Pritchard. Try and behave yourself and keep your nose clean. If you know what I mean.'

He tapped his own not inconsiderable hooter but Keef was bursting to leave the cop shop.

'I'm a reformed character sergeant. Given up sex, drugs and annoying the neighbours.'

'Christ, that must 'av been a tough five minutes.' The sergeant tried to sound sympathetic.

'Ok ok. Just let me out and you won't see me for dust.' Keef was escorted to the exit and left. As he stepped outside a guitar case was thrown after him. Immediately a dust storm obliterated the pavement in a cloud of yellow haze. Inside the sergeant turned from the window.

'That toxic chemical plant must be leaking again. Give the ministry a call Williams.'

Keef Pritchard was having a welcome home party. He sat in the Black Cat Inn with two mates and feasted on vodka and crisps. One of the lads apologised.

'Not exactly caviar is it?' Keef took the cue.

'So when are we going to Russia, Mick?' The other mate chimed in.

'Next week. East European fans are dying to see us and we've got all sorts of deals going on.'

Keef warmed to the idea and pointed to his luggage.

'Ace or should I say Kalashnikov...and I'll tell you what. That guitar in there'll be a handy spare. We could even use it for a bit of trade. The Russkis haven't got much in the way of top notch rock gear. They'd pay handsomely for that with premium Ukrainian White.'

The trio toasted each other.

'RASPUTIN !!!'

On the other side of town a large car was pulling up in a dark alleyway.

Sticky pulled out some money wrapped in a bundle. He put his head in the passenger compartment.

'Some guys I'm working with want to stock up on the sauce. They'll need cheering up while they're away from home.'

Cousin Vasseline took the cash.

'They say money only brings misery. Mind you with money you can afford it. Give them this latest batch of satan's syrup. That should give them the tonic they deserve.'

Vasseline handed over a carrier bag and then put pedal to metal. Sticky just had enough time to withdraw his head before it was almost torn off...again.

SIXTEEN

In the enormous private library in St Petersburg Van Hellbent Junior sat alone. He was feeling depressed because he'd been researching for days with no result worth mentioning. An arm settled on his shoulders and great Aunt Olga smiled at him lovingly. Van Hellbent Junior leaned against her soft breasts.

'I can't find anything that helps great aunt. It's the end of the road, I'm a failure and I've let the family down. I feel like I've thrown a stone into the air and missed,' Van Hellbent rubbed his chin. Olga stroked his hair.

'I vill let you into a family secret. As well as zis vast library my father also had a secret room. That iz where ze most valuable and most rare papers are kept. Come viz me my child.'

Olga moved off and Van Hellbent Junior followed her zig zagging past huge cabinets and piles of books to the end of the vast library. Olga slid away a panel that Hellbent Junior thought was a window. His great aunt then revealed a secret door bearing the legend. THE REALLY STRANGE DEPARTMENT. Van Hellbent broke out into a smile.

Near Red Square in central Moscow, Keef and The Bones pushed their way through a hotel foyer. The group were besieged by Russian fans and Rasputin freaks. The Brit rockers and a few Slavonic groupies were quickly chaperoned into a large lift. A couple of the roadies made it to the same elevator with their suitcases. One of the roadies was Sticky. As the lift reached their floor the band and groupies went in one direction and the roadies in the other. The hotel had been built in the late 1940s in the monumental style preferred by the Soviet hierarchy. It looked just like the government offices on the other side of the street except that this building had bedrooms. There was an attendant on each floor ostensibly to help the guests but also to monitor the comings and goings on each corridor so that the goons in security would have something to do.

Sticky entered his room and thought he had just stepped into an early film set. There were several shades of brown on the furniture, carpet and walls. Oddly appealing thought Sticky but then he had a flashback to his caravan back home and decided he was actually in the lap of luxury. Here at least he had his own toilet and a telephone. The latter rang. It was Keef.

'Psst mate...I need you to do somethin' for me.' How could Sticky refuse?

'Er...oh hi Keef...Mr Pritchard sir.'

'My room soon as you can,' barked Keef.

Keef's groupie was taking a live goose out of a cardboard box as Sticky walked into the suite. Sticky thought the accommodation was definitely a notch or two up on his own. There was a separate bedroom for a start and the paintwork was obviously not from the same factory catalogue. Keef pointed at the horned guitar.

'I want you to take this junk and offload it in exchange for fifty jars of top notch Ukrainian White Horseradish. I don't want any of that second-rate shit the crew are using. That's just chalk. This guitar's a spare see and I need the genuine sauce to keep me perky in this god-forsaken place.'

Sticky narrowed his eyes as he looked at the guitar.

'I had one a bit like that once...'

HONK HONK

Sticky's attention turned to the Russian groupie. She was stroking the neck of the talking goose in a suggestive way. Keef interrupted his stare.

'Now go on...don't hang about. We're playing in a concert

96

tomorrow night and if I don't get a fix soon I'll be in a hell of a state.'

Sticky picked up the guitar and made for the door while Keef turned to his new lady friend.

'Ludmilla, put that goose in the bleedin' bathroom girl before it craps itself and when you've done that I've got a little job for you in the bedroom.'

Later that night Sticky stepped out into the street. He was well wrapped up against the cold because the temperature was a mind numbing minus twenty degrees centigrade. There might not have been much to numb in Sticky's case but he wore a woolly hat just in case. He walked up the short hill from the hotel and passed St Basil the Blessed's Byzantine cathedral. He'd never seen a sight as enchanting. The onion domes in bright coloured stripes were lit up and the building dazzled him. Its shapes were interwoven and resembled flames leaping out of a bonfire. Sticky thought it bonkers and beautiful and even blessed it seemed. He rubbed his head barely able to weigh up his predicament in this city. He was in a strange land and it was time to trade.

He crossed over a square that looked as though it had seen its fair share of major events and walked part a closed department store or perhaps it was an old palace. It was difficult to tell at night. Sticky walked on for a block and the street lights started to diminish. Now there were just pools of light that were well spread out. He turned a corner and saw a few characters lingering about in doorways. It looked like a possible black market hangout. He wasn't wrong. He took up a position between two other dealers who eyed him up suspiciously. Sticky didn't look or smell like a militia man or cop so they ignored him.

Back in the warmth of the hotel, Keef and Ludmilla were

proving that the frosty relations between East and West were just a political hiccup. When people got this close together who cared about tomorrow. Ludmilla was very dark with olive skin and had feline green brown eyes that were probably the result of some central Asiatic blood. She lay alongside Keef and tilted her head back and closed her smouldering orbs.

After a moment she felt his lips touch hers. She opened her mouth then slowly pushed her tongue into his mouth. She felt his muscles tense up as her tongue met his. Their breathing got deeper. Keef squeezed her shoulder and purred.

'Start me up little sister.'

She stroked his arms, his waist and his thighs. Keef moaned with pleasure. He moved his mouth and found her breast. Her nipples were erect under the starched fabric of her blouse. His lips closed over one nipple and she felt a sensation as intense as if he had cut into her. She gasped. A Western fashion magazine lay on the bedside table! As Keef went down in front of her and lowered his face she delicately picked up the copy of Vogue. Keef found the hem of Ludmilla's skirt and lifted it. He moved forward and kissed her right there in the middle. Her breathing was shorter now. It was the turquoise dress and matching shoes on page thirty four that really excited her. After she'd examined all the details, including the price, Ludmilla put the magazine down as gently as she could. Then, slowly and expertly she slid a hand to Keef's zipper and pulled it open. He closed his eyes as she explored his size with her fingertips. She pulled at his pants and he knelt in front of her. She leaned forward and opened the buttons on his shirt and sucked his skin. He wanted to be inside her quickly. He put his hand between her legs. She was swollen and wet and his touch was like a velvet wand. Keef lowered himself and she felt him enter her.

'Push hard,' she said 'I vont you so much Keefski.'

He began to move and she heard herself give little gasps of joy every time their bodies rubbed. Moments later Ludmilla felt she was falling out of the sky as she caught sight of Keef's bulging wallet on the coffee table. It made her whimper. Suddenly she felt his body shudder and she shook with expectant pleasure.

As punters walked by Sticky opened his coat in flasher fashion. One or two citizens jumped back in surprise. Most of them were after cheap perfume or American cigarettes. After a couple of hours Sticky had had enough. He was freezing and no one seemed interested in the guitar. He noticed that some of the hawkers had gone inside a dimly lit bar at the other end of the street. He thought he would try his luck there.

By the time he managed to open the firmly sprung door whose powerful hinges kept it firmly shut against the cold Sticky felt a little weak. It took him a few seconds to adjust to the orange glow and smoky atmosphere inside. He dragged himself to the bar and looked around. It was quite full and he felt the eyes of the locals were on him. He was obviously an outsider. Having failed to attract the attention of the barman he was wondering what to do next when an old man approached him. He was tall and thin with whispy white hair and most of his teeth were missing.

'Eeenglish?'

Sticky tried to reply but his jaw was still frozen. He neither nodded nor shook his head. He did both. The old man was confused.

'Er...Dutchman...Swedish?'

Sticky just managed to identify himself with effort.

'Wwwelsh.'

'Ah like Merlin ze magic one. Ha...velcome to Russia my friend. Velcome to my country.'

Then he lowered his head so that only Sticky could hear.

'You know here vee have plenty of danks but no soap powder.'

Sticky was loosening up

'Danks…er sorry er I don't understand?'

'Boom boom rat a tat boom boom.'

'Oh tanks. Oh yeah. Yeah plenty of tanks.'

The old man was waiting. Sticky offered to buy some drinks.

'Well dank you yes dank you,' smiled the old man.

He turned to the barman and asked for two large vodkas. He was acknowledged.

'You vil have to pay in dollars or your Welsh pounds,' said the old man.

Around them there was just the clink of a glass to provide atmosphere when suddenly a man in a dark box like suit appeared and moved from table to table. The old man turned to Sticky.

'Dat man is asking people to put out der cigarettes. It's a liddle strange. Someone important must be comink.'

A pale blue car pulled up outside. It was a limousine and Sticky could tell it was an American motor, a Cadillac maybe? The door opened and an entourage walked in and occupied one of the larger tables that had been cleared of low lifes. Glasses and bottles were provided and some pickles and sausages were brought in. Amongst the group was a large fat man with hair that was obviously dyed.

'It's a group from ze American embassy. Some of zem enjoy ze bohemian side of Moscow. Ze man with zem is big opera singer. He was flown in for de entertainment. They maybe have diplomatic evening at embassy and now they vant to relax.'

Sticky was impressed. Whatever bush telegraph operated here was damned impressive. As Sticky looked on at the new arrivals a door from the kitchen opened and one of the waitresses came out holding a balalaika, a local triangular shaped guitar of sorts. She was focused on the embassy group and strode towards them playing and singing like a trooper. It was a folk song guessed Sticky and she sang it with confidence and no mean talent. It was obviously meant for the opera singer who smiled all the way through her performance. The waitress delivered a genuine heartfelt homage to the great one or so it appeared to the Welsh roadie. When she finished playing she disappeared as quickly as she had appeared. The American group clapped, flashed a few dollars and then continued chatting and drinking.

'It's for him dat people have stop smoking. De man with painted hair. Dey vant to protect his voice,' said the old man.

Sticky thought how unpredictable life in this city must be. It was a total mystery to someone like himself. He sipped his vodka. It was in a chilled glass but as he felt the spirit run down his throat it warmed his insides. He noticed that his elderly companion wore a coat and suit even greasier than his own but he also had a stained yellow tie with horse head motifs.

'So how's the cavalry doink?' said the old man.

'Better,' said Sticky and gestured that they should have two more drinks.

The old man raised his hand at the barman..

'Not many girls here tonight er…' said Sticky. He wasn't looking for a hooker, not yet anyway but it seemed like the right kind of bar room talk. The old man beamed.

'Boris Orlov at you service. More girls here on Saturday nights. Ha! you have somedink between your legs…Yes?'

Sticky was suddenly unnerved.

'Hey what's your game. I'm not here to be picked up old man.'

'Of course not my friend. I vos looking at ze instrument under your coat.'

'Oh that,' Sticky quickly flashed Boris a view of his guitar.

'Trying to sell it. Don't suppose you're interested?' he said in a lowered voice. The old man laughed.

'No my friend. You have come to ze wrong part of town. Ze young person market is in another place. Here is money exchange, American cigarettes, country girls and sometimes goose paté.'

Sticky sighed and sipped his vodka.

'So what do you do…er Boris?'

'Ha! I was engineer but I had too many correspondences with friends in west so I was forced to leave job. Ze are very security conscious in Russia but we learn to live wiz it.'

'Were you always an engineer?' Sticky was warming to Boris.

'Oh no no. I was professional soldier first. Ha! I remember ze old days when I vos in sixteenth lancer regiment. One day our Colonel ran to our barracks very excited and told us telegram arrived. He wave it about and tell us a beautiful Countess iz going to visit us.'

Boris put on his Colonel's voice.

'Prepare yourselves and your mounts for ze guard of honour. I vant this regiment looking very smart. Ze best horses ze best uniforms and by tomorrow mornink!'

Sticky nodded humouring his companion. Boris continued in his own chuckling voice now.

'So I vent to shine my horse and my god! As I brushed him he grows between his legs ze biggest sausage you ever saw. A real champion.'

The old man stepped back acting out the moment.

'Ha…so I jump and say…So who got ze telegram you or ze colonel?'

The old man cackled manically. Sticky smiled politely. He had heard better punch lines.

'I tell you he was a real crazy horse. He should have been in ze movies. Ha unfortunately, one hard winter I had to eat him.'

Sticky looked towards the sausages on the American table. He was about to order some food but changed his mind.

An hour later Sticky stumbled back to the hotel. Even though it was just a few minutes walk the temperature seemed much lower than before. His spirits were at rock bottom. The bill in the bar had been huge. Much more than Sticky had expected. It almost cleaned him out and he had failed to trade. He was still stuck with the guitar and he did not feel like chasing around an unfamiliar Moscow looking for a sale. He reached his hotel room floor and walked down the corridor nodding at the babushka who dozed on a chair. She might be bored but at least she was out of the cold he thought. When he entered his room the heat from the radiator wrapped itself around him. It was just what he needed. He lay down the guitar on a small couch and threw his coat over it. He sat on the edge of his bed, thawed out and stared at his surroundings. His room was being used as a storeroom by the band members. They had considerately left their amplifiers up against his wardrobe. Sticky was thinking of shifting them to one side when there was a knock at his door. It was a light tap tap.

'Christ…that Keef's got a nerve,' thought Sticky. He shuffled to the door and opened it a little. He had a surprise.

'I am Svetlana. Maybe I keep you company?'

Sticky looked at the tall attractive blonde. She had the pale blue eye shadow that so many of her countrywomen used and she had very red lips. Svetlana wore a short skirt and white blouse opened at the front. Sticky figured this was not the hotel manager. He was tempted but remembered he had blown all his money in the bar.

'Er..don't suppose you take credit?'

103

'Maybe you have ze English cigarettes? Vee could talk if you prefer?'

Sticky let her in but he was nervous. Svetlana walked over to the bed and sat down.

'Vee can talk first,' she said taking command of the situation.

'Tell me about himself?'

Sticky was numb and remained by the door. He'd never seen anyone as beautiful as this woman of the night.

'Are you musician maybe?' Svetlana purred.

'Huuu…rrffhhhhh gobs wahnttt.' Sticky was stumped and his legs turned to jelly.

Svetlana tried again.

'Do you know how much Polar bear weighs?'

Sticky tried again.

'Gnibberrrrrr lommsss….NO.'

'Neither do I but it break ice. Yes?' Svetlana crossed her legs.

Sticky could feel his shyness fading a little. He moved towards the bed. Svetlana looked into his eyes as he approached.

'The vv...voices in my head have told me to sit next to you,' he said in a very high pitched squeaky voice. There was a swish of fabric and she took off. Sticky closed the door and felt empty. He was still stuck with Keef's guitar, he was broke and he would be alone again tonight. He paced about and stared out of the window onto the Moscow scene. There were few lights on this side of the hotel. He had a view across the black river to a factory of some sort with a barely discernable mural of Lenin on one wall. He looked over his shoulder at his coat sprawled over the guitar. He was restless. After a night like this he could not just lie down. Too much was going on in his head. What was to become of him? He looked back at his coat. Sticky could resist it no longer. He dragged an amplifier away from the wardrobe mirror then turned to his coat and threw it over the bed. He picked up the guitar plugged it in and draped it over his body.

'I could've been a contender Mister Keef, *the riff,* Pritchard. I could enjoy pulling Ludmillas and Svetlanas, having roadies do all the dirty work and having me name in all the rock magazines. I could be great....if I could play a bit.'

He dragged his fingers over the strings and nearly fell back in amazement. It sounded beautiful. He strummed some more and the strings seemed to dance under his finger tips. A melody flourished under his hand. Within moments he was producing expert string bending routines. It was incredible. Sticky couldn't really play before. He was the kind of roadie who did the heavy work. It was left to the others to tune up instruments if asked. Sticky was amazed and his spirits soared.

As he got carried away he paraded around the room. He even sounded like Keef doing a fancy lead break. Just then he thought he heard a moan from somewhere. He stopped for a moment and listened. All he could hear was the chugging from the radiators. What the hell he decided to carry on. As he passed the mirror on the wardrobe door he glanced up with a rock sneer. He saw himself but where was the guitar? His jaw dropped. He looked down. The guitar was still hanging there but when he looked up in the mirror again all he could see was himself and his arms outstretched and empty. But they weren't empty. He looked down and the guitar seemed to have risen up to his neck. Sticky's door flew open.

'What the bleedin' hell is going on here then? What are you still doin' with that guitar. I thought I told you to get out there and trade it for some stuff. Apart from which how are me and Ludmilla supposed to get it on with you doing an impression of one of those talent show gits.'

A goose honked in the background. Sticky felt naked.

'Er... nobody wanted it Mister Pritchard. All I was offered were a few boxes of stale fags and some funny coloured tights. And I nearly froze to death.'

'I don't care if the snowmen were howlin.'

Keef lifted the guitar up to Sticky's chin.

'You're both a bloody waste of space.'

For the next two days the band attended a number of press conferences and radio interviews around Moscow. The authorities seemed happy to have The Bones playing to large audiences despite their anarchic reputation. After all they would usefully divert young Russians from more subversive activities. The real threat to national security came from disgraced scientists, writers and academics looking for a political platform but not from these rockers. These young men wore velvet, they had a romantic poetic look and they were only musicians. They sang of Armageddon and hell fire but these were just metaphors. The band enjoyed the theatricality of danger but not danger itself surely. For God's sake these boy men had not even done their national service!

While the band were on the press circuit Sticky was at the concert hall. He was helping to erect the sound system and scaffolding for the main stage. Everything was different - the plug shapes, plug holes, plug sizes, the sockets, the wiring and the food. After a late meal of badger goulash and thick beetroot soup Sticky got back to his hotel room. He was tired and could not decide if he would be going out again. As he crossed over to his bathroom he froze. He heard a tremulous glissando soaring from one pitch to another in one continuous arc. He approached the source of this beautiful music. His succulent fingers were drawn to the guitar. He picked up the instrument and he was immediately energised. His fingers fanned the strings and were propelled through a medley of dance tunes from sixteenth century galliards and baroque gavottes to minuets played at one hundred miles an hour. Sticky was in raptures, despite the pin pricks of blood that dropped from his hand, he was in ecstasy. The night music changed his mood.

There she was. Sticky could see her near the lifts. She must have been patrolling these corridors most evenings looking for lonely businessmen. He wanted to taste Svetlana. She could read his thoughts. She recognised his hunger. She forgot about the voices in his head. He wanted to be with her and tonight he would pay any price. Svetlana entered the bedroom.

'You need...'

He raised her wrist to his mouth. A drop of crimson stained her skin. She felt a shiver running through her body. She didn't normally feel that way with a customer especially one like Sticky. He looked like a loser the other night but something had changed. She could see it in his eyes. The sensation she felt was thrilling. She felt moist. The perfume of sex and power was about this match. Sticky guided her to his bed and turned the lights off. Now he could be anybody.

He began kissing her body, pulling at her clothes and licking her breasts. She felt him running his teeth over her skin. They were sharp. She meant to retaliate by giving him a scratch but he squeezed her body tightly and she was almost breathless. His tongue darted in and out of her mouth like an electric cobra. Then she felt his hand pulling at her skirt. She moaned because he was as hard as iron and filled her to the point of pain. She panicked as a feeling of tearing and stabbing began to take over from the sensuousness she felt earlier. These sensations were not happening between her legs. She looked wide- eyed at the man above her. Was she allowing herself to be consumed? She tried to push him away but he was too strong. His lips burned her neck and she felt his teeth sink in to her flesh. His tongue lashed her veins and she started to feel light headed. She felt a trickle of liquid running down her back. Everything was turning from dim to black. Sticky drank and then her arms fell against the sheets. Her heart had stopped.

When Sticky woke up the next morning he panicked. He had not found a dead woman in his bed before. Svetlana looked so serene but it was clear she was no longer alive. He could tell from the blood-stains on the pillow and the coldness of her body. He was scared too. My God what happened? Was it the Ukrainian sauce? If it was why could he not remember taking any? He shot out of bed and was about to phone reception and report a murder or death or something when he heard the tinkle of guitar strings. It was like a morse code. He instinctively understood the message. ***Don't do it.*** Slowly it all dawned on him.

Sticky squeezed himself and an equipment trunk out into the corridor. The large black trunk had wheels under one end just like a suitcase. As Sticky pushed it towards the lift his eyes were filled with tears. He cried all the way through the descent and he sobbed as he crossed the foyer. When he stepped outside the hotel he put on some sunglasses to shield his eyes from the daylight. He took Svetlana to the concert hall.

The snow had eased but the streets were dirty and slushy. Trams criss- crossed over the roadways and pulled up outside the Centre Rock 'N' Rollski. It sounded more Polish than Russian but the place was built in the spirit of Slavonic brotherhood. The word Bones could be recognised among the Cyrillic letters that dominated the billboard. Russian fans poured into the centre.

Once the concert got going, The Bones played their set in style and dazzled the Russian crowd. A pale looking Sticky watched in the wings holding onto his red and now glistening companion. Suddenly Keef threw off his usual Telecaster guitar and rushed towards his knackered looking roadie and grabbed the horned instrument. He ran back with the red guitar and started kicking out and strutting at the edge of the stage. He drove the fans wild. The band started to knock over and smash up their own equipment. It was all the rage in the West but the crowd here were horrified at the damage to so much good kit. Never having seen such wanton waste the fans soon became excited by the public display of aggression. This was revolutionary behaviour. The Russian audience started raising their fists in salute. Young girls felt a thump thump sensation in their lower body. The young men started pushing against the bouncers. The lights flashed across the crowd and they started to feel they were part of the performance. Their cries and shouts taunted the band to excess. They got paid in a rising torrent of rock sounds that were barbaric and creative, artistic and divine, powerful and passionate. The crowd started to feel the feral excitement and the security people started to move in. That was Keef Pritchard's cue.

He raised the horned guitar over his head and slammed it down like an axe. There was a spurt then a torrent of red liquid. The guitar body broke up and the crowd went berserk then hysterical as the stage became awash with blood. Sticky screamed,

'Let it bleed!' but nobody heard him.

Before the security men could do anything a miasma erupted from the liquid, a noxious fetid vapour that produced a smell so foul that everyone began to choke and gag. Pandemonium followed and there was a rush for the exits. Keef collapsed and his band mates made for the wings. Sticky who was not affected by the fumes went backstage to the large trunk he brought from his hotel. He gently lifted up Svetlana's body and then placed her by the front row of seats. He kissed her forehead tenderly. Hearing some voices at the back of the hall Sticky could just make out the silhouetted figures of the fire brigade in their gas masks. He moved as fast as his tormented body allowed him. He salvaged the damaged guitar. He saved his master.

The next day a western news reporter stood outside the Centre Rock N Rollski. He addressed his crew with a piece to camera.

'No one knows where the blood came from but in cold war Russia strange things can happen…and do it seems. Staring into the abyss of extremist forces, many people are predicting the second coming of Ivan the Terrible to rid the country of….'

A Militia man moved in to stop the recording. He was backed up by a number of colleagues in army uniform. They were large men with Mongol like features. These were Russian conscripts from the central Asiatic territories. The TV crew backed down and moved off.

On the St Petersburg to Moscow express train, Van Hellbent Junior read a newspaper and occasionally glanced out of the window. The view was of unending snow covered fields, undulating plains and occasional birch forests. Every twenty miles or so a village would mushroom out of the earth. The houses were all built from wood and had heavily carved decorative windows and sagging roofs. He could see how a landscape like this would throw up incredible stories and some desperate history too.

Despite his high hopes the really strange book department at aunt Olga's was mostly dedicated to extreme occult studies. The Hermetic Orders, The Builders of Azarah, The Temple of Dark Light and Rodent Rouge were just a few of the organisations and sects he looked up. He was certainly drawn to the mad bestiary of that there was no doubt. There were crested snakes, half human half monster - all terrors, the woodcuts by Hartman Schedel with their headless bodies and faces on torsos and other weird characters that medieval minds described as being of diverse shapes and marvellous disfigurements. They all exerted fascination but gave no answers. There was also a massive section on biological racism, Nazi cults and fascist iconography which Olga had provided. The SS badges and insignia designed by Walter Heck and the Hugo Boss uniforms were ultimately just a dreadful distraction. Despite the setback, Van Hellbent Junior was still convinced that he would find a missing link in this part of the world. As a personal treat he was planning to visit the Izmaylovo market in Moscow on his way home. It usually had some interesting artefacts from pre revolutionary days. Genuine antiques could still be found there and Van Hellbent wanted a particular icon. If he found the Angel of the Golden Locks he would be a happy man. The real thing was from the twelfth century but he hoped to buy a good modern copy.

He adjusted his seating position, turned over a page of the St Petersburg Times and lurched forward. There was a report of The Bones concert in Moscow. Damn it he had missed his favourite band. But this was no review it was a news story. His attention was drawn by the bold headline, **IT'S ONLY ROCK N ROLLSKI!** and a photograph of someone he thought he recognised. It was an anaemic and withered looking roadie holding up a guitar covered in thick electrician's tape. Van Hellbent stared at the picture. Where had he seen that face before? He focused on the guitar too and its image began to trigger something in his brain. He read on…

'Cleaners trying to wash blood off walls…three fans trampled to death….lead guitarist revived…the band thrown out of the country…returning to Britain today.'

Van Hellbent Junior knew he had to catch a plane from Moscow's Domodedovo airport as soon as possible!

EIGHTEEN

A car with flashing blue lights pulled up outside one of Wrexford's police stations. The uniformed driver got out with a bag of sandwiches and entered the building. Inside an interview room, Van Hellbent Junior stood next to his suitcase.

'Glad to see you looking so well Inspector.'

Smollett was back at his desk.

'Thank you Professor...I reckon someone had spiked my tea. A most unfortunate episode but everything seems to be alright now. Except for the five unsolved murders and a blood-stained ballroom in Russia that's straining diplomatic relations.'

Van Hellbent held up the crumpled newspaper he had bought in St. Petersburg. He pointed at a photograph.

'This is your man Inspector. A roadie called Sticky. Find him and we will find the answer to our problem. Now look at the shape of that guitar. Look at the small horns of its body. Look at them very hard.'

Smollett shot up from his chair.

'It's the mark on the victims necks! My God I think I've handled that cursed instrument myself and never realised.'

Van Hellbent filled in the blanks.

'There was hysteria in Russia when The Bones played there. But how much of it was induced by the evil power of the guitar. I'd say ninety percent. This is unique in the annals of vampire study. An apparently inanimate object with a taste for blood. Sure there's been fiction involving cars and other weird contraptions but this is a case of the undead taking over the power of music. The power that can take us outside of ourselves and turn us into angels or devils.'

Smollett briefly regretted not having gone to university.

'But hang on. Why didn't the victims become vampires too?'

'Because Inspector, it's virtually impossible for humans to become blood sucking guitars.'

'Oh yes.... of course. Right then, we'll put out an all points bulletin on this Sticky character and he'll lead us to the evil one or thing!'

At the ancient university, Professor Vasseline was in his lab alone. He turned a tap on an elaborate looking still with spiral shaped tubes. A creamy fluid started to flow out.

'That's it. My finest sauce yet. This will match the stuff coming in from the East. I'll soon have enough money to last me a lifetime…unless I buy something.'

Across town the blighted caravan park looked more desperate than ever. It was raining hard and most of the residents had to stuff ear plugs or tissues into their ears to protect them from the drumming sound of the rain on their roofs. The cheapest, saddest and most decrepit of the vans on the site had all but deafened its inmate. Sticky did not care. He had other things on his mind. His eyes were like the rings on an old electric cooker. Concentric circles of pain and ugly corroded darkness. Behind Sticky the horned guitar lay on an old sofa. It had a few glue marks and a little crazing from the breaks it suffered on stage but otherwise it looked little the worse for wear. Which is more than could be said for the man in front of it. Sticky was sat on the floor carving some wood. A chair in the corner of the caravan had its seat missing. Sticky was using it to form a shape of some kind. As he sculpted the wood with a cut-throat razor he had found in a drawer he nicked his finger. Damn! He grimaced with pain but carried on. Behind him he heard a slight moan and sensed some movement. His eyes flicked to the wall mirror and he saw that the sofa was empty. Sticky turned slowly and saw the guitar was still there…but nearer. He turned back to the mirror and sure enough the sofa was empty. He carved more quickly.

Outside in the rain-washed car park a police car pulled up outside the site owner's office. Police Constable Williams darted out of his vehicle and ran inside the building. Williams showed a photograph of Sticky to the man in a trilby hat who knew all the residents on the site and nodded when he saw the picture. He stepped towards his office window and pointed in the direction of a small shabby yellow caravan.

The guitar was almost touching Sticky's back now but he carried on carving at speed. Chunks of wood flew from the old seat and bit by bit a definite shape started to emerge. Double damn! In his haste Sticky cut himself again and blood ran from his finger over his work. Behind him he felt a definite shove in the small of his back.

Underneath the caravan in a subterranean world of tunnels a badger family had created a labyrinth of passageways. The den was two metres below ground and the space immediately below Sticky's mobile home contained the bones of long dead badgers and part of the skeleton of Sir Lancelot Walters Wynn. Over the last twenty four hours the badgers had been disturbed by an occasional dull red glow that seemed to come from the deep earth itself. It pulsated then disappeared and it caused them to dig even more tunnels to escape the strange light.

The phone rang in Van Hellbent's chambers. It was the police. Smollett provided the vital information. They had found their man.

'...a caravan site in north Wrexford.'

Van Hellbent Junior swallowed hard then got a grip of himself and provided instructions.

'It's vital that you keep your men back. And don't move in until I have given you the all clear. We're dealing with unimaginable powers of evil here and unless we synchronise everything there's no telling what this thing might unleash. Above all…I must be ready.'

The two men were responsible for the future of mankind. Inspector Smollett realised his hour had come. He assigned four hit squads all of which had a firearms expert attached. He articulated his objectives to his staff and defined his command and control options to his superiors. He had one last thing to say to his team in this moment of huge risk.

'Right men…and women. We must not turn our back on this danger and try and run away from it. If we do that the danger will double but if we tackle it head on without going weak at the knees we will reduce the danger by…er…a lot. Good luck everybody.'

A figure in a duffle coat crept out of the university chemistry building and pulled the hood around its head to shelter from the rain. A mechanical groan then a roar made the hooded figure look up just as an enormous tipper truck shed its massive load. The figure screamed and the hood fell back enough to reveal the Horseradish King. In an instant the truck load of hard round things completely buried Professor Vasseline permanently.

In his oak panelled chambers, Van Hellbent Junior prepared himself for what he knew would be a career defining confrontation. His study looked like the closing down sale in an ecclesiastical supply shop. Crucifixes, prayer beads, bishops hats, bibles with embossed crosses, Van Hellbent had the lot. As he rummaged around making sure he had not forgotten anything there was a loud and urgent knock. Bramble the university porter put his head around the door.

'Excuse me sir but there's an articulated lorry load of garlic blocking the Principals office at the moment. The driver left a note saying the load is addressed to you ...sir......sir?'

Bramble could see that it was pointless continuing.

'I beg your pardon sir..!'

Van Hellbent was standing by his window. He was in a trance. Beyond the window a large pyramid mound of giant garlic clumps were piled up in the quadrangle near the chemistry building.

Sticky finished carving. Oddly his ears were beginning to look like tiny horns. He turned to the guitar which was now resting on his shoulder. As he stood up the guitar wavered. Sticky raised the giant plectrum he had made and raised it high above his head. The plectrum had a sharp tip which was pointing downwards. Sticky was breathing deeply. He needed all his waning strength to do what was in his mind. He wanted to plunge his carved plectrum deep into the instrument that he had suffered too much for. The guitar wailed and started to play itself. An incredible demonstration of guitar playing virtuosity. Sticky hesitated.

'If you could play like that for me,' he croaked, 'You'd make me a star. Cos all I can do is play on people's nerves.'

The guitar answered him with a tingling sound that was so beautiful that he almost collapsed. Sticky could resist it no longer. He dropped his giant plectrum and took the guitar to his body so that its magic would penetrate his very being. Instantly the wires wrapped themselves around him and drenched the guitar with fresh blood. The breaks and cracks that had previously scarred the alder body were now restored. It was in rude red health again and it wailed with joy and the tremolo arm vibrated with pleasure. Wah wah wahhhh.

Van Hellbent Junior woke from his trance and found himself within fifty metres of Sticky's caravan. The rain had stopped. Hellbent was dressed in stage rock gear. A fringed white leather Perfecto jacket, ripped jeans, cowboy boots and the bandana on his head almost completed the look. The crowning glory was his pure white Fender Stratocaster guitar. The door of Sticky's caravan flew open. A gaunt Sticky and an immaculate red guitar emerged. Van Hellbent Junior stepped forward a couple of paces.

'I recognise you despite your bloodless pallor… you're Sticky. I am your Nemesis.'

Sticky wobbled a little. His hands had turned red and his ears had changed into horned tips just like his guitar's. Van Hellbent thought he might be drunk or worse. Sticky certainly sounded like he was.

'Well, I suppose you fancy yourself as a wizard on the guitar? Thing is… I can out play anyone with the help of my bloody friend here.'

'Oh yeah,' Van Hellbent sneered.

'Oh yeah,' Sticky sneered back.

Van Hellbent whispered to himself

'What am I saying. I've hardly played a guitar in my life'.

Sticky advanced a little.

'Okay…I challenge you to a duel. The last man to keep playing wins.'

Van Hellbent was desperate. He had not thought it would come to a musical fight. He brought his guitar along as a prop. He had no intention of playing it if he could help it.

'Couldn't we have a garlic throwing competition instead?'

The red guitar wailed in profound disagreement. Van Hellbent bit his lip. He drew blood. The red guitar screamed with fury. Suddenly the heavens opened and Van Hellbent was bathed in a bright white light. A moment later the ground opened up in front of Sticky and a hellish red glow illuminated him from below. Van Hellbent still hesitated.

'Well maybe then…'

Behind him a deep techno sound kicked in. He turned around. The world's largest Marshall amplifier stack was backing him up. Van Hellbent Junior beamed.

'Right you're on.' He produced a golden plectrum and fanned his strings.

Sticky growled in response.

'Terror, mayhem, chaos…my work begins'.

The duel started with Sticky and Van Hellbent exchanging licks. Each successive riff was faster and more complicated than the previous one. As the flurry of fingers on fretboards reached a rate of unparalled speed and dexterity the high volume and pitch became excruciating. Sticky's caravan shuddered with the material cracking sound levels. The caravan park itself began to tremble.

The police arrived and Inspector Smollett climbed out of his car. He was immediately assaulted by the guitar tsunami, stuck his fingers into his ears and ducked down to avoid the worst of it. The duel continued

Above the battle, in the block of flats that overlooked the caravan site, one of the residents was getting particularly upset. An elderly woman was woken up from her nap by the din. She rose from an armchair and walked towards the slightly open window. As she passed the mantelpiece she glanced at a photograph. Two old ladies stared back at her. They were dressed in identical woollen coats, wore identical hats and held matching handbags. They were twins, Lillian and Lucille Girl. One of them was the cleaning lady who was murdered in the Grande Theatre. The old woman looked towards the window and complained to the photograph.

'It's them bloody noisy lads Lilly. They don't give us no

peace since you went. No peace at all. It's gotta stop.' She wrung her hands.

'Oh I wish you were 'ere to sort them out. They play their music mornin', day and night. They got no consideration. What's the world comin to?'

As the duel continued the old woman opened up her balcony door. She stepped out and pushed aside her washing line. She looked on the scene below and returned inside. Considering she was hard of hearing the noise was more of a nuisance than a pain. To the residents in the immediate area the sound was off the scale. They all had their hands clapped over their ears. Smollett gritted his teeth as he watched Van Hellbent duck walk around Sticky. The two virtuosos were constantly trying to out do each other.

It was Sticky's turn and he spun round three hundred and sixty degrees creating a circular furrow as he bent the strings further than any musician had ever done.

The old woman returned to her balcony. She was carrying a large bucket of water mixed with her secret washing up liquid recipe. It had been gifted to the twins's ancestors by gypsies in exchange for hospitality at a time of danger to the travellers. Barely able to stand in the hurricane created by the amplified sound the elderly woman forced herself to heave the bucket onto the edge of her balcony wall.

Two metres below Sticky's caravan, the badgers were blinded by the intensity of the red light that was sending its beams to the surface. There was no escaping it. As if that was not bad enough some black serpent like creature was moving about in the den. Not being well up on electrical power lines the poor badgers mistook Sticky's devilish amplifier cable for a monster worm. One that could feed the family of fifteen badgers for a month or more. Partly crazed by the light and confused by the electrical serpent, which on the one hand could fill up the larder or threaten young cubs on the other, the badgers decided to attack.

Up above, Van Hellbent was not going to wait for Sticky to stop playing before he delivered his killer punches. The pair of them drove each other on in a slapping, stabbing, shrieking contest of distortion and feedback alternating with beautiful moments where the notes danced about as if created by musical gods.

As Sticky produced some more screeching sounds the old lady could stand in no longer. She tipped her bucket over the pair of duellists. Most of it fell onto Sticky and the open ground around him. Simultaneously the badgers, using their pointed canines and jagged molars, bit, tore and crushed Sticky's electrical cable, which as it happens carried one hundred thousand volts. The combination of this energised electrical power and the special water short circuiting the exposed metal parts that the badgers revealed caused the horned guitar to explode into a thousand fragments vaporising Sticky in the process.

Inspector Smollett was bent double as he ran towards Van Hellbent who had reached the point of deafness. Smollett shouted.

'That's the most incredible thing I have ever seen or heard. You've been hiding your light under...'

BOOM

An enormous bang ignited Sticky's caravan and the flames took the shape of a flaming guitar when seen from the point of view of Lucille Girl from her high balcony.

Smollett hurriedly escorted Van Hellbent to a waiting ambulance.

The flames carried on their deadly dance and the ground within the contours of the fiery guitar shape began to crumble and collapse. The caravan soon sank and then disappeared from view and the badgers decided to emigrate pronto.

Inside the ambulance Smollett could hardly contain himself.

'Well, that's hopefully put paid to the forces of the horned one. I should think we're both due a commendation for today's work Professor. Perhaps even the Nobel peace prize for you.... or would you prefer the MTV award for best newcomer?'

Van Hellbent Junior still had the ringing guitar sound in his head.

'I'll ssettle ffor aa ffluffy ccloud...'

Smollett leant nearer

'What's that man? Speak up!'

NINETEEN

Sidestepping some road works, a family crossed Wrexford high street and walked into Guitar City. A mother, father and a beautiful girl with curly blonde hair looked around the displays. Drum kits, shiny brass instruments pianos and guitars in all sorts of shapes and colours filled the showroom. There were pictures of guitar heroes on the walls. It was as if the ghost of Gordon Jones had a hand in the design of the store. A salesman approached the family. He had a vague resemblance to Sticky but of course that was just a coincidence because Sticky was dead. Anyway the salesman was smartly dressed and immaculately groomed which Sticky never was. He expertly ushered the family towards his desk.

'Ah…Mr and Mrs Lloyd, sorry to keep you. I've worked out the repayments on the items you mentioned with regard to your daughter. Now let's sit down over here and I can take you through the figures.'

As her parents got down to business the teenager wandered through the store. When she passed a rack of guitars her eye was caught by a red instrument that looked brighter than all the others. It reflected light like nothing she had ever seen before. As she moved closer she heard what sounded like a fairy's breath on its wire strings. It was a secret whisper that captivated her. Without even realising it her hand stretched out and reached towards the guitar body. The girl spoke softly and adoringly.

'You're beautiful…we were meant for each other.'

The guitar moaned expectantly and the girl was drawn closer.

As Van Hellbent Junior was shaken from his latest trance he saw his reflection in a shop window opposite the road works. He was dressed as a showgirl in a skimpy glittery costume and high heels again! Except this time he wasn't serving drinks he was operating a pneumatic drill. He looked around and for some reason he couldn't quite fathom he started to walk towards a music shop.

Meanwhile in the guitar factory on the other side of Wrexford, Moira Jones, who was Gordon's widow, was overseeing the latest batch of raw guitars coming off her production line. Each one of them had a red stain through its body.

'It was a bloody big alder tree,' she said to herself.

HOW TO TURN THE BOOK INTO AN INDIE FILM

The film version will begin with a night exterior of a house in a suburban street. Music floats over us as we approach the windows. The music will be the kind that accompanies the closing credits on a Quiz programme...rather jolly. We cut to an interior with an old radio and realise that this is the source of the sound. A hand appears and hovers over a copy of the Radio Times before it flicks through a couple of pages. A long fingernail slides up the page to identify a new show. The radio is then tuned into another station to pick up the broadcast of... The Roadie's Vampire Guitar.

The descriptive details and background would be delivered by a narrator and the dialogue would be performed by a cast of eight actors playing out various roles. Both these elements would be filmed in an apparent radio station. Occasionally, we would cut in a shot of a location or a short piece of action. These shots could be a dark alleyway or a tree bending in the wind or the exterior of a theatre. Just a hint of illustration.

Close up shots of the demon guitar being played would be intercut with the story as required. The killer guitar would be revealed by recording the action of the wire strings unravelling at various speeds but in supreme close up. That's one way of doing it. The actors performances and editing would take care of the rest. Colour, shape, speed and the timeline would deliver the thrills. This is not an animated production but the film would have a lot of pace. It needs that kind of feel.

One element that is not in the main story would be a band of dedicated "listeners". These characters would be filmed in different environments listening to the show on their radios.

Ranging from a cosy domestic interior, to a warehouse night shift, to a call centre, to a mansion house, to a long distance lorry driver, these lives would connect with the main story just like you dear reader. Except of course, this being the film version, some of these apparent "listeners" might not be all that they seem.

CONTACT **info@vampireguitar.com**